Puppets in the Attic

R. S. RAYBORN

ARCHWAY PUBLISHING

Archway Publishing books may be ordered through booksellers or by contacting:

Archway Publishing
1663 Liberty Drive
Bloomington, IN 47403
www.archwaypublishing.com
1 (888) 242-5904

Interior Image Credit: R Sanchez

ISBN: 978-1-4808-8841-8 (sc)
ISBN: 978-1-4808-8842-5 (e)

Library of Congress Control Number: 2020903466

Print information available on the last page.

Archway Publishing rev. date: 2/29/2020

This book is dedicated to the loving memory of
Rachel Ann Lusher,
who was the inspiration of Amelia one of most animated,
fearless and funny characters in this story.

Contents

Prologue

When creation was finished, the mix of life on earth was very complex. Carnivorous animals occupied the same space as delicate ferns and gentle herbivores. It became apparent that there was a need for a sweet, wholesome, and loving purity in nature to balance the aggressiveness that was there.

Fairies came to be, and before long, were providing their wonderful presence all over the planet. The variety of fairies was endless. Among them were passion fairies, throbbing with the passion of life's gentleness and love. There were also garden fairies, white socks fairies, tooth fairies, snow fairies, wayward fairies, nocturnal fairies and protector fairies and on and on.

Most fairies lived in colonies led by a chosen, highly qualified matriarch. The colonies were self-sufficient, with many skills and talents represented and the experience of the elders to guide the young. The fairy hamlets and colonies were very productive, successful, and happy democratic social enterprises.

In a low, mountainous area, the Beaver Valley colony thrived. A kindly old man lived there, enjoyed an affinity with nature and the children he loved. His desire to create something special for his grandchildren was the beginning of a history-altering adventure.

The lovable old man was known by most people simply as Grandpa. Grandpa enjoyed making things—toys, furniture, and even small dolls. His favorite thing was to make things from wood. The woods where he walked and often collected downed branches had a wonderful aura of mystery and life. Grandpa always said a few words of thanks when he found wood he considered special—oak, sycamore, maple, and aromatic cedar. Those pieces seemed to have life still in them and received reverent attention as he did his work. The pieces he made all seemed to have a special lifelike quality.

One especially cold winter after a very blustery storm, Grandpa went out to pick up branches the high winds had blown down. He was on a search for dry firewood and limbs to carve. Grandpa made the best solid wood furniture, tools, and toys in three countries, maybe the whole state! He was very selective about the wood he gathered for carving. "You see," he would say, "Firewood can be any old wood. But carving wood must be special, like having a personality. I feel like its spirit speaks to me." Grandpa's long experience in life and his friendships with the local Indians taught him to respect nature and to understand the natural cycle of life. So Grandpa never cut a healthy living tree down unless it crowded the other trees and it's removal was necessary. He would prune his fruit trees or cut a diseased limb off since this would only help the tree. He just never cut a whole living tree down unless the forest was overcrowded. Grandpa preferred to use dead trees still standing or live trees that had fallen down. When he could not find downed trees, he would pick up the branches and limbs that had fallen prematurely.

He claimed that the local Indians taught him how to feel the life forces coursing through a tree. They told him that the creaks and groans he heard at night before he fell asleep were the trees talking to each other.

He often swore he could hear the trees' lullabies wafting across the dale. The Indian called them "tree spirits" and told Grandpa he honored the trees by helping to protect them. They said, "With your creations, you give the trees a second life." The songs he heard were the tree spirits' little helpers thanking him for being good to Mother Earth.

It was no wonder the sadness he felt on this walk when he came across a freshly broken live oak tree. It was rotted at its base and had broken in the force of the high winds, which blew the night before. The sorrow he felt for the tree drew him to touch the broken trunk lying on the ground. He ran his hand along the bark and knots. He felt a burl that looked like a nose. It made him chuckle. For a brief moment, he almost thought he saw a big, old, bearded face gracefully sleeping the day away. Grandpa gathered the broken branches and parts of the trunk as a vision formed of the dolls he could create. He wondered how he might create the new personalities and how they could entertain his grandchildren. As his thoughts expanded, he could almost hear the children's laughter while the dolls danced. While the fantasy was strong in is mind, he went into his shop and began to create.

After Grandpa left this life, his spirit combined with the spirit of the wood and seemed to live on, honoring him and all he believed.

The adventure begins! Readers, open your minds, relax and enjoy!

CHAPTER 1
The Attic

It was a stormy day. Down a little-used country lane was a sad-looking, old, two-story house. It had the look of not having been lived in for many, many years. The paint had faded to a stained gray, and the shutters had either fallen off or were askew on their hinges. The railing on the front porch was falling apart, and the stairs were in a shambles.

The front door was left open partway, and many leaves littered the floor inside.

In the family room, old furniture damaged beyond repair still sat where it had been abandoned. Dingy, moldy drapes hung over the windows, casting a dreary, shadowed light into the room. Along the stairwell, what had been a beautiful floral wallpaper peeled away from the wall. Upstairs, lighter-colored areas along the wall outlined the places where photographs and paintings had once hung.

On the second floor, past the bedrooms at the end of the hall, was the door to the attic. Two windows illuminated the attic and helped dispel the gloom surrounding the many things stored and forgotten in this lonely space. Beside a standing mirror was an open trunk with many labels of the places it had been plastered on it. Paintings leaned on boxes and hung from walls. A wagon, a tricycle, and many other old toys were scattered from a really big box that had been tipped on its side. Old musty clothing and blankets were piled here and there.

On the floor near one of the windows sat a toy theater box. Along the back wall hung two marionettes, a boy puppet and a girl puppet.

They once were special hand-carved Christmas presents for a little boy and a little girl from their Grandpa, who loved them dearly. But that was a long, long time ago.

"Opus, are you awake?" Felicity, the girl puppet, asked.

The boy puppet curtly answered, "Yes."

Felicity dreamily reminisced. "Oh, Opus, won't it be wonderful when our loving children come home to play with us?"

Opus was feeling surly this stormy afternoon. Bad weather always seemed to put him a poor mood, and today he felt especially testy. Marks on the back wall, too numerous to count, showed the many seasons that had passed. Because of the passage of so much time, he felt that Felicity's usual dreamy and optimistic nature had made her lose touch with reality. Basically, he felt she was disconnected from reality, and at this moment, he did not care to be nice. "Don't count on it. We've been hanging around here so long we're falling apart," he responded, irritated.

Opus's right eye was stuck closed. Felicity looked like she needed a dolly doctor. Her dress was shabby and dusty. Her right hand had fallen off at her wrist, and mice had stolen all of her beautiful brunette hair.

Feeling downcast, Felicity replied, "I know, Opus!" She sniffled. "But dreaming of when we played with the children makes me happy."

Crash! Tinkle, tinkle. A branch crashed into the window next to the theater. Felicity screamed as glass and debris showered the area. The storm raged out side, and cold wind and rain blew through the hole in the window.

Felicity was scared and shivered. She jumped with fright when lightning flashed and thunder clapped. She reached out for Opus with her handless arm, and when she couldn't grasp him, she started to cry.

Opus snagged Felicity's arm and held it protectively. "It's okay. It's just lightning. Look, a branch has broken the window." He pointed to the right of the theater box, where a broken branch lay among glass and leaves. In all their time in the attic, they had never seen a storm so violent. A gust of wind loudly rattled the window. The noise made the puppets look up just in time to see two dark shapes blow through the opening in the window. The dark objects were blown all the way to the back wall of the attic, where they thudded hard against the wall and fell behind the trunk.

"Oof, ugh," came the sounds from the shadows.

The sound of the wind and rain died away, and for a moment, the attic was eerily silent. Shaking Opus's hand to get his attention, Felicity whispered, "Opus."

"Shhh!" Opus replied as he pulled Felicity close and whispered in her ear, "I think the wind blew in a couple of birds!"

They held each other for a moment and just listened. Rain started to fall again, and all they could hear was the pitter-patter of drops on the roof.

Opus and Felicity were afraid of animals. All their experiences with them had turned out badly. The puppets had learned not to move by themselves in front of the children or any other living creatures. They had not wanted to scare the children because the puppets loved them so. They didn't move around animals because the puppets were afraid of being eaten. That was why Felicity let the mice steal her hair. Over the many seasons, the puppets learned how to protect themselves. After tolerating the squeaking nuances till bored, they pulled pranks on the mice. Without being seen, Felicity would tweak their tails, or Opus would flick their ears. When a mouse felt the touch, it would jump, look around, and scamper off, wary of unseen stingers. Opus and Felicity had never experienced birds, so they didn't know what to expect. Behind the trunk, in the shadows, there was a shuffling noise and then another loud thud.

"Oh," Felicity peeped.

From the shadows the puppets heard a loud whisper. "Be careful! This is a noisy giant's dwelling, like I've seen in drawings. Look how huge everything is!"

With the sound of voices, Opus's eye widened with surprise and anxiety. He urgently whispered, "Act natural." And they broke their embrace and went limp.

In their nervousness, the puppets had forgotten they were made of wood. When their limbs and bodies fell into relaxed positions, they clattered noisily.

"Did you hear that?" Came an excited whisper.

"Yes, it came from over there," answered another voice.

A moment later, a pair of eyes and a pert nose peeked out from around the corner of the trunk. The eyes disappeared for a second. Then a pretty little girl with short, black ponytails and small wings emerged. She tugged and pulled a second little girl into view behind her.

The girls stood there side by side, holding hands and nervously looking around the room. They were wet from head to toe. Drops of water dribbled on the floor as they shivered from the cold.

The second little girl, also with wings, had short, curly, strawberry-blonde hair and cherub cheeks. She wore a short, green, jumper dress. She spied a small, tattered teddy bear on the floor next to her, picked it up, and held it tightly for protection.

The first little girl had a curious yet mischievous look on her face. She wore a greenish halter top and what appeared to be flower petals for a skirt. She took a tentative step forward. The little girl pointed at the puppets with her free hand, turned excitedly to her friend, and exclaimed, "Look, Tulip, over there. Noisy giants!"

Tulip let go of her friend's hand and hid behind her. She peeked over the other girl's shoulder and after a good look asked, "Aren't they kind of short to be noisy giants?"

Being the brave one, the first girl crept toward the little theater box. Tulip followed close on the heels of her friend and did her best to stay hidden behind her. As they neared the stage, Tulip spied Felicity's broken hand on the floor and picked it up.

While Tulip examined the hand, Opus and Felicity had a chance to look at the little girls. *Gossamer wings! Like a dragonfly on a dewy day*, Felicity thought. *How beautiful.*

Up close and out of the shadows, the puppets could clearly see the transparent wings that sprouted from behind the girls. Still wet from the rain, the wings shimmered in the waning light.

Tulip turned Felicity's hand over, and as she studied it, she said, "They only look like noisy giants." She paused, and gazed up at the puppets. "They're made of wood, see?" She offered the hand to Amelia, her friend, to inspect.

Amelia grasped the wooden hand, looked it over, and saw the frayed end of a string at the wrist. The delicate fingers had mouse-sized tooth marks on them. Amelia fanned her wings, rose up, and hovered in front of Opus. She scrutinized his head and carefully touched the lapel of his jacket.

Tulip, who was already apprehensive, gasped as she watched Amelia take the wooden hand and knock it on Opus's forehead.

Even though Opus was irritated, his curiosity kept him still. He didn't know what to make of the small girls with wings, so he endured the annoying treatment.

"Don't do that," a frightened Tulip whispered. She shivered in fear and hid behind the tattered bear. "You're going to make 'em made at us," she warned.

"Mad at us? You scaredy frog! They're not even alive, see?" And Amelia knocked harder on Opus's forehead, causing it to bob back and forth. Opus could hold his composure no longer and winced.

Tulip thought she saw the wince and buried her head in the bear's back. She pointed at Opus from behind the bear, and in a muffled tone said, "He moved!"

Amelia stared at Opus. He remained stock-still with a stupid look on his face. "Aww, come on," She said indignantly. "You're such a scaredy frog. You jump at the tiniest bump in the night thinking it's some warty old troll who's going to jump out and get you!"

R. S. Rayborn

Tulip peeked around the side of the bear and saw Amelia standing with her arms crossed. She had landed in front of Opus and was leaning against him without fear.

Amelia taunted poor Tulip with the three words no youngster could let go unchallenged. She pointed at Felicity and said, "I dare you to come up here and touch that one!"

Tulip's eyes went wide with panic. "I, I, I don't want to. Um, um, I might get a sliver! You remember my last sliver. It was huge, and there was blood everywhere. And remember? I fainted dead away." She frantically embellished and babbled as she hoped the excuse was good enough to satisfy Amelia.

Amelia just grinned mischievously at her. From the time they were fledglings, growing up in the same nest, they had been the best of friends. Amelia loved her little nest-sister dearly, but she was not above teasing her. She knew all the right buttons to push to get shy little Tulip to come out of her shell.

Amelia impishly danced around and sang out her favorite taunt. "Scaredy-frog, scaredy-frog, scaredy-frog, Tulip is a scaredy-frog."

Irritated and indignant from the taunting, Tulip glared at her friend. She was getting so angry, you might expect steam rising from her bright blonde hair. With an angry, determined look, Tulip held the bear, put her fists on her hips, and leaned forward as she stuck her tongue out at Amelia and went, "Braaack."

Amelia just tittered, crossed her arms, and gave Tulip an overly, wide-eyed, "I dare you," expression, which, in a way, said, "Well?"

Tulip stomped her feet, and with a shake of her hair, harrumphed, "Ooohh!" She growled and then stomped up the stage to Felicity.

Felicity tried not to laugh at the comedic drama unfolding in front of her. She thought, *the little imps! Well, I'll show them.*

Tulip stood next to Felicity and tried to stare Amelia down. Without looking, she reached up to touch the wooden girl's face.

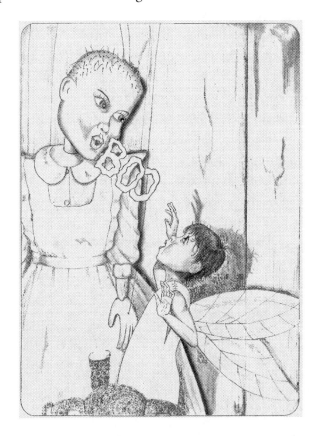

"Boo!" Felicity puffed loudly as she reached toward Tulip.

With the sudden move, a terrified Tulip fell backward, hard upon her rump. Thump! When she landed, a cloud of dust poofed about her. *Aachoo,* Tulip sneezed

With a yelp, fearless Amelia fluttered to the highest rafter, leaving only a puddle of raindrops where she had stood.

Opus, with his arms akimbo, glared at Felicity. They hadn't moved in the view of anything since that vicious little Rover attacked them many years ago.

R. S. Rayborn

Felicity laughed hysterically at the sight of a wet and disgruntled Tulip. Tulip, resting on her bruised bottom at that moment, didn't appreciate the laughter.

Opus's irritation melted away. With Felicity's infectious laughter and the sight of the dust bunnies floating around Tulip, he started to laugh too.

Obviously, Tulip was very unhappy. She was scared, wet, dirty, and cold. On top of all that, the wooden noisy giants were laughing at her. "Stop it! *Achoo!* It's not funny! *Achoo!*" She tried not to smile, but it didn't work. The mirth and happiness were affecting her too. First she tittered a little, and then she snorted. And that made her giggle. Soon she was laughing right along with them. *Achoo!*

In such a scary situation, the laughter she heard seemed strange to Amelia. But she screwed up her courage and peered over the edge of the rafter. What she saw astounded her. All three characters by the theater were laughing with glee.

Amelia was still a little wary, but she figured anyone who laughed like that couldn't be all bad. She fluttered back down and landed near Felicity. Upon landing,

Amelia caught Felicity's attention and with the laughter subsiding, she smiled up at her.

"Hello, little one," Felicity said. "And what might your name be?"

Still holding the wooden hand, Amelia pointed it at herself and said, "I'm Amelia," and reached out with the hand to greet Felicity.

Felicity stretched out her handless right arm to Amelia. When the separated hand met Felicity's wrist, they both smiled at the connection. They shook hand, arms, and bodies. This started a new round of giggles between them. While Felicity and Amelia were bonding. Tulip picked herself up from the floor, tried to dust herself off but only managed to smear the wet dust on her clothing and face. She looked up and caught Opus smiling at her. Shyly, with her hands behind her back, Tulip eased over to him. She looked down timidly and held out her right hand. "I, I'm Tulip."

Opus accepted her hand. But instead of shaking it, he did a little bow and kissed the back of her hand. Tulip gasped in surprise, blushed a beautiful, embarrassed pink, and giggled coyly.

Opus did not let go of her hand as he made introductions. "How do you do, Tulip? My name is Opus, and this lovely lady is Felicity."

"We are blessed to meet you," Amelia said with a curtsy.

Tulip sighed deeply as she held Opus's hand and gazed up at him with puppy eyes.

Felicity reached for one of Amelia's wings. "How beautiful," she said.

"Oh, please be careful. Our wings are strong, but they can still be damaged," Amelia explained.

"What are you?" Felicity inquired. You're not birds, insects, or human. You're kind of a combination of all three."

"We're passion fairies of the fey, or enchanted people from Beaver Dam Valley," Amelia answered.

"Fairies? Enchanted?" Felicity looked bewildered.

"Oh, yes, Felicity. Do you remember the picture book of fairies Mother showed the children at bedtime?" Opus asked brightly.

Felicity's eyes widened with excitement as she realized what they were. "I remember. They're just like the tree spirits in Grandpa's stories."

R. S. Rayborn

Amelia piped up, "Well, I can see that you are made of wood from trees, but why do you look like noisy giants? And why are you all tied up like that?"

"Noisy giants?' Felicity asked. "Opus, do you know what noisy giants are?"

"No, I don't. But whatever they are, we must look like them," Opus answered. Then he addressed the little fairies. "To answer your question, Amelia, we are tied up because we are puppets."

"Pup-its?" Tulip sounded out. She still looked a little bewildered. "I don't understand."

"Well, we were carved out of a branch from a tree by Grandpa. Then he gave us to his grandchildren puppeteers," Opus explained. "Yes," Opus continued matter-of-factly, "our loving children would play with us by moving our strings. The strings lift our bodies, arms, and legs, and make us move."

"Opus," Tulip anxiously tugged on his hand, "Are the chel-dren gonna come and play with you soon?"

Thoughtfully he answered, "No, Tulip. We have not seen them for many, many seasons now."

"You are the first living things we've ever talked to," Felicity said. "And I must say, it is quite an experience."

"Normally we don't move in the presence of other living creatures. Especially after what happened that first Christmas morning," Opus explained.

Felicity picked up the story. "We awoke to smiles and hugs from a little girl and a little boy. They hugged Grandpa and thanked him. Then they put on the shows with us. Then they stopped and opened up all sorts of presents, toys, clothing, and books. But we were their favorite toys, and the children were so happy."

"Then Uncle Bud came by," Opus said, sounding annoyed. "He smoked nasty ol' cigars and dumped ashes all over the place. His present was as big as the theater box, and something was whining inside." Opus looked to Felicity, who took a deep sigh and gestured for him to continue. He grimaced. "It was a new puppy. It was half-grown and into everything. It wasn't able to get at us, so it wrapped its paws around the children's new dolls and stuffies. There were body parts and stuffing everywhere! The puppy was caught teething on a dolly's leg."

"It was horrible! I've never been so scared," Felicity said, shivering from the memory. "The puppy growled and acted like it hated us, unlike the children, who cared for and loved us. After the dolly massacre, the dog was put back in the box and never allowed around us again."

Tulip asked Opus, "How do they move your strings?"

"Like this." Opus grabbed the string to his right leg with both hands, and with a little effort, lifted it. He let out an exhausted breath as he let go. "Whew! It seems we've been growing weaker day by day. So it's kinda hard for us to move on our own now."

"I can help you move," Tulip piped up. She let go of Opus's hand and leaned the bear on the back wall of the stage. Tulip fluttered up the stage wall and landed on top of Opus's strings and heaved. She grunted, "Fummmnagh," as she strained. She tried and tried to lift him, but after several tries, Tulip said, "You're just too heavy for me!" She glided down to the stage floor and retrieved her bear with a hug.

"That's okay, Tulip. It's just so great to have new friends we can talk to," Opus said appreciatively. "It's been forever since we've seen any living creatures, and it's been lonely. Even the mice have gone away."

Felicity looked off dreamily and said, "I so miss playing with our puppeteers. We would do slapstick, and the children would laugh and laugh." She had a burst of inspiration. "You don't need to move our strings for us to entertain you," Felicity said brightly. "We can tell stories and sing. And even though we are not as strong as we used to be, we can still do a little soft-shoe dance."

Opus, with a big smile, said, "That's a great idea. Would you like us to put on a show for you?"

In unison, the fairies answered excitedly, "Yes, please."

Then Amelia held her palms out to the puppets and asked, "Could you wait a moment, though? We need to build a nest. It's getting late, and it's awfully cold. We need to build a nest before it's too dark."

"How thoughtless of us! By all means. Feel free to use anything you wish. Our home is your home." With open arms and a bow of his head, permission was given.

The industrious little fairies smiled and curtsied a thank you and set out gathering the softest clothing and fluffiest material they could find.

While Opus and Felicity planned their show, they sneaked peeks at the fairies as they built their nest. Finally, the fairies finished the nest. It looked warm and comfy.

"Amelia," Tulip said anxiously, "it's gonna be dark soon, and we won't be able to see the show."

"We need some kind of fire or torches," Amelia said.

The fairies fluttered over to the boxes and opened them up. One large box looked promising, and they dived in.

The puppets watched with great interest as they heard rustling and thumping within the box. Wads of newspaper, tissue, and baubles came flying out.

"Aha. Found some candles and holders," said one voice.

"I think I found some chimneys too," came the voice of another from the box.

The fairies brought over two candles, candleholders, and glass chimneys. They set up the candleholders on either side of the stage. Then they placed a candle in each of the holders.

Amelia produced a piece of flint and steel. Sparks flew as she struck them together at one of the candlewicks. When sparks landed on the wick, Tulip blew softly and made the sparks glow brighter. They worked well as a team, and soon, "poof," a flame ignited.

Tulip produced a dry twig and lit it. She carefully shielded the flame as she flew over to other candle, and set fire to its wick.

Working together, Amelia and Tulip placed the glass chimneys over the candles. The lamps illuminated the entire stage. The warmth of the candle's glow lightened the many years of gloom that had dominated the puppets' home.

All Opus could say was, "Wow!"

Felicity beamed at the fairies for their ingenuity.

"Well, that's much better. Come on, Tulip." Amelia started to crawl into the nest.

"I'll be right there." Tulip tossed the tattered bear toward the nest, and while the bear was in flight, she flew to a shelf up over the theater.

Tulip did not see the bear bounce off Amelia's back and fall into the nest.

"Hey, whatcha want this stinky old thing for?" Amelia sounded kind of irked, until Tulip flew back down with an armload of stuff. "Oh," Amelia said with understanding.

Tulip dropped a small spool of brown thread, a small pair of scissors, and three potpourri sachets. Then she took a needle she was holding and stabbed it into the side of the nest. Amelia was snuggling in as Tulip climbed in and snuggled down beside her. Tulip used a piece of flannel pajama to wrap around herself, sat the bear on her lap, and readied her sewing kit to repair the bear. The scent of the sweet sachets drifted up to Felicity and sparked memories of Mother telling the children bedtime stories while she sewed. Inspired by her memory, she urged Opus, "Let's tell some stories of our adventures with the children."

Opus smiled. "That's a great idea!"

The sky cleared as the night progressed, and moonlight shined through the window. The fairies sat enthralled while the puppets regaled them with stories, song, and dance. Soon one of the candles burned out. The other was close behind.

Opus was in the middle of singing a sweet lullaby when Felicity touched his arm to get his attention. "Opus, look. They're asleep. Don't they look like little angels?"

Opus smiled as he gazed upon the two little fairies snuggled warmly in their nest. "Yes, they do. And they look like our darling children used to look after a long day of fun."

Tulip clutched the small, repaired teddy bear and sucked her thumb. Amelia was wheezing softly, and every time she exhaled, her wings gently buzzed.

"I believe we have found two wonderful new friends. Good night, Felicity."

"Good night, Opus."

As the last light of the candle flickered out, they fell fast asleep to sweet dreams.

CHAPTER 2
IT'S A NEW DAY

Opus was having a wonderful dream. He was onstage in a nightclub, crooning to Felicity.

They both were dressed for performing, and love was in the air. As he sang, he gazed deeply into Felicity's eyes. Suddenly, she biffed him on the forehead with the palm of her hand. She hit him so hard, he fell flat on his back. Then things really became weird. A gaggle of girls screamed his name and rushed on the stage. One enthusiastic girl with strawberry-blonde hair sat on his chest and repeatedly whacked him on the forehead with his microphone. Each time she hit him, she chanted, "Opus, Opus, Opus." The whacks hurt, and he blinked with pain each time he was hit, until …

"Blink, Opus. Are you awake? Blink!"

Opus realized that he had been dreaming, yet the pain was real. After a moment, he realized he was being rudely awakened by a knocking on his forehead. When he finally opened his eyes, there was Tulip, hovering in front of him with a big cherub-cheeked smile upon her face.

She hovered there patiently with her hands behind her back and smiled. "Good morning, Opus."

With such a sweet greeting, he could not be angry with her. He yawned and stretched. "Good morning, Tulip. It's so wonderful to wake up to your beautiful smile."

Her heart aflutter, she blushed at his words, being called beautiful! She grinned coyly at him. Bubbling with enthusiasm, she asked, "Are ya hungry?" Out from behind her back, Tulip brought two live termites and offered them much too close to his face.

Opus cringed and put up his hands to ward off the termites. "Tulip," Opus entreated but didn't take his eye off the squirming bugs.

"Yes, Opus?" Tulip responded with pure adoration.

"Y-y-you do know termites ee, ee, eat wood," he stuttered nervously. "Um, he looks hungry," he said, pointing to one of the termites as it gave him the raspberry.

Tulip turned the hand he pointed with and looked at the struggling termite. Then she held it back out to him again and asked, "Wanna squish it and get some revenge?"

"No, no! That's okay. Just please get rid of it," Opus pleaded.

She shrugged and popped one termite and then the other into her mouth. Chewing around the termite bits, she said, "Wow, I'm hungry. I'm gonna go get me some more." And away she flew to a darkened corner of the attic.

Opus could hear the little fairies as they hunted and ate termites.

"Look, I found a big one."

"Mine's bigger. Munch, munch, munch."

Felicity stared at him, wide-eyed with a constrained smirk on her face. She couldn't hold back anymore and burst out laughing.

"What's the matter with you?" Opus asked. He was still unnerved by the termites, and Felicity's laughter didn't help.

Wickedly she said, "We have termites in the attic! It won't be long before they come to eat you up. Look!" She pointed behind him dramatically, all wide-eyed and serious. "They're coming to get you. Brooha ha ha!" She finished with a sinister laugh and wiggled her fingers at him, trying to be all scary and such.

"Don't do that! You know how much I hate termites." He gave an involuntary shiver and groaned. Felicity fell into hysterical laughter.

In the middle of her giddiness, Felicity spelled out what had happened. "When Tulip offered the bugs to me, I told her I like my termites roasted." As she spoke, she plunged into more fits of mirth. "But, but that you liked your termites fresh and wiggly." Felicity wiggled her fingers at him again. There was no containing her now. She was having so much fun. "Then I told her you would be so grateful for a fresh termite breakfast."

Aghast, Opus said, "No! You didn't."

"Yes, I did," she said with an impish look upon her face. "And your new girlfriend, eager to please, promptly rushed to awaken her sleeping prince. Oh, what a treasured surprise she had to give him!" Felicity finished, smugly satisfied with herself with the look on Opus's face.

"Girlfriend?" Opus asked, confused and highly perplexed.

"She has a crush on you. You don't see it 'cause you're a guy," she told him in that know-it-all big sister way that girls sometime use. Then, with a lot of flips of her hand and rolling of her eyes, she prattled out, "You so wowed her with your sophisticated ways. She has been all gushing, and goo-goo eyed since!"

Defensively, Opus said, "I've been nothing but a proper gentleman."

Felicity responded, innocently batting her eyes, "That is very appealing to a young lady."

"Oh, no!" Opus said with a worried look on his face.

"It's okay. Crushes happen." Felicity patted his shoulder with her handless arm. "Just keep being her friend, and when a truly handsome, hunky, younger man comes along, she'll forget all about you. Then she'll follow him around like an adoring puppy." Felicity stared in his eye, very seriously and sad. "Just do me a favor, Opus. Don't break her heart."

Opus sighed with visible relief. Then he screwed up his face with a thought and stared at Felicity.

When Amelia spoke, termite bits and goo oozed out of her mouth. Yuck. "We hab tube leeb room." She then turned and called behind her, "Oowip, get uffingor face." She took a swallow. "We havea long flight ahead, and you don't want to weigh yourself down." Chew, chew, swallow. "Remember what they say: 'A fat fairy flies no further than it can be thrown.'"

Reprovingly, Felicity said, "I don't mean to be motherly, Amelia, but hasn't anyone taught you not to speak with your mouth full? We could not understand a word you said." Felicity lifted her apron and roughly wiped her cherub cheeks clean.

Amelia quickly recovered from her clean up and apologized. "Oh, I'm sorry. Umm, we havta go. We've been gone all night, and our clan will be very worried about us. Especially after that terrible storm yesterday."

In shock, Tulip looked up with termite goo dribbling down her chin. She just realized what Amelia had said and whined loudly. "I don't wanna go!" Then she grabbed her teddy bear and flew over to Amelia. Tulip made her biggest doe eyes at her and pouted.

Amelia knew Tulip's trick all too well because she taught it to her. So she put her foot down firmly. "No, Tulip. We must go home!"

"Whaaaa!" Tulip started wailing. With her arms wrapped around her bear, she stomped her feet and threw a royal tantrum.

Amelia was unmoved. She knew her best friend would eventually understand and forgive her.

Felicity was not used to such emotional outbursts. With her heart ready to break, she scooped Tulip up and hugged her tightly. "It's okay, honey," Felicity said soothingly as she kissed Tulip on the top of her head.

Tulip held up her repaired teddy bear. "Berry needs a kiss too!"

Felicity smiled and gave Berry a kiss on the nose. She then wiped Tulip's face clean.

Opus was already missing the bug-eating little angels when the sound of a car coming up the driveway made them all freeze.

They heard the *thunk* of a car's doors closing, and Amelia flew straight to the window to look out. She saw a tall, fat, well-dressed man walking toward the house. A waif of a woman in a long overcoat trailed behind him.

The man had a purposeful stride and seemed very impatient. Passing through the front gate, he did not hold it open for the lady like a gentleman was supposed to. He just slammed the gate behind him, as if the lady was not even there, and strode up the front porch.

The woman, on the other hand, seemed dainty and caring. She fixed some rose vines and stopped to smell the flowers. As she passed through the gate, she carefully closed it behind her.

As the people disappeared under the roofline, Amelia turned to her friends and exclaimed fearfully, "Noisy giants!" She flew back over to her friends. The fairies held on to each other and trembled with fear.

The puppets didn't understand the fairies' reaction. They chatted excitedly with each other about the possible return of their family.

Felicity asked with hopeful expectation, "Opus, do you think it's our children come home to play with us?"

"I don't know, Felicity." Opus was apprehensive as he listened for the humans' approach.

Creak! Bash! Clatter! They all jumped at the sudden loud sounds from below. They remained deathly still as they strained to hear the people moving around on the first floor. Worried, Amelia tugged Opus's coat for his attention. When he finally noticed her, she whispered with a panicked look on her face, "Must hide!"

Tulip hugged Felicity really tightly and said to Amelia, "But I don't want to leave them unprotected!"

Felicity squeezed Tulip. "It's okay, little one. We'll be just fine!" After she assured Tulip, Felicity raised her eyes to Opus with her own worried look.

Opus glanced furtively around and saw what he was looking for. He pointed to a dark corner high up. "There! Where the rafters join together, there's a good hidey-hole."

Amelia let go of Felicity and flew straight up to inspect the hideout. She quickly reappeared with a cloud of dust trailing after. "It's perfect, but dusty. Come on, Tulip!"

Tulip felt safe nestled in Felicity's skirts. She clutched her bear tightly and whined, "But Berry's worried they won't be safe!"

Amelia put herself nose to nose with her little friend and said, "We're not safe! Remember what happens when noisy giants see us. Opus and Felicity know noisy giants and lived with them."

Tulip remembered the stories they heard. She was embarrassed as she recited what she had learned from Solomon like a shy schoolgirl: "Nutty noisy giants never stop trying to grab naughty little fairies who know not to be seen."

"We'll be fine, Tulip," Opus assured her. "But you need to go hide yourselves quickly! And remember, be quiet."

Felicity grabbed Amelia's arm and said, "If our family has come to take us away, just know it is so wonderful to have met you. I'll never forget you."

Thump! Bang! Startled, they all looked up when they heard the attic door smack the stairwell wall.

"Go," Opus urged and shooed them off toward the hidey-hole. Then he turned to Felicity and implored, "Please, whoever they are or whatever they do, don't move this time!" Felicity nodded. Amelia flew straight and quick to the hidey-hole.

Tulip pulled her bear close and whispered, "It'll be okay, Berry," as she slowly followed Amelia up to the rafters. As Tulip pushed her way into the hole, a pile of dust poured out and drifted to the floor.

Opus and Felicity watched as the man and woman appeared at the top of the stairs. When they reached the very top, they walked right into Tulip's dust cloud.

"*Achoo,*" sneezed the woman. "This place is sure dusty."

"Gesundheit! Here." The man shoved a handkerchief at the woman.

"Thank you." She took it and honked her nose loudly.

This was not Mother or Father. Opus and Felicity went limp and made a slight rustling noise.

"Did you hear that?" the lady asked fearfully.

Unconcerned, the man responded, "Probably just mice."

"Mice!" She looked around nervously. "I wish I hadn't worn a dress."

"I told you we were going to look at a house," he said gruffly.

"Yes, but you didn't say it was out in hick country, rundown, and falling apart," she argued.

The man ignored her comment. He moved a few boxes around and did a cursory look into an old trunk filled with dresses. "More junk," he said with distaste.

Still worried about mice, the woman carefully inspected the contents of some of the boxes. Almost everything she saw was musty, smelly, and dilapidated. As she rummaged, she asked, "What do you want to do with all this stuff?"

He was pondering a handful of old photos when he said, "Just leave it. The fire and demolition crews will reduce it to ash." He callously dropped the pictures to the floor. "Then they'll bulldoze the ash and debris into a hole and cover it. It'll be like this place never existed."

A cold draft of wind hit the lady and made her shiver. Looking for the source of the draft, she spied the little theater box, walked over, and picked Felicity up by her strings.

"Poor old thing. Left here unloved and forgotten." She turned the puppet to and fro and studied the workmanship. "Too bad it's not in better shape. It might be worth something."

The man glanced over her shoulder at the puppet. "It's ugly," he said.

She gave him a sour look and went on studying the little treasure. "Oh, I'm sure it was very lovely when it was brand new. All she needs is some hair and a little TLC." The woman gently caressed Felicity's cheek.

"Drop it!" The man demanded. "You don't need more junk." He then kicked the fairy nest, which flew into pieces.

The lady gently set the puppet back into the theater box, where Felicity and her strings slumped to the floor.

There was a soft shuffling sound. Then a very tiny, *achoo.*

"There's that noise again. This place must be crawling with mice," the lady commented. She shivered and looked around nervously, hoping not to see the hidden creepy-crawlies.

The man looked a little nervous himself. "Yeah, mice. Let's get outa here." He turned on his heel and beat a hasty retreat to the stairs. The lady took one last, longing look at the puppet. She heard another noise and quickly followed him down the stairs.

The puppets heard the man's voice fade as the humans descended the stairs. "The crew will be here this afternoon to start the burn. Then heavy equipment will …" His words trailed off as the couple left the house.

Amelia buzzed right to the window and watched the noisy giants leave.

An anxious Tulip fluttered straight to Felicity and hugged her tightly. "Are you all right? Berry and I were so scared for you."

Felicity sat up and returned the hug. "I'm fine, Tulip. The lady actually was very gentle and seemed to care about things. But oooh, that man!" Felicity clutched her arms around herself and shivered with dread as she thought about the gruff noisy giant.

Opus just hung in limp dejection. He felt totally beaten as his world was beginning to crumble around him.

Tulip, seeing that Opus was sad, reached over and shook his pant leg. "It'll be all right, Opus. Amelia is really smart. She'll think of something."

After watching the noisy giants leave, Amelia zoomed back down, and with a hard landing, started a vigorous tirade. "How dare they?" She paced back and forth. "And to use fire! Don't those noisy giants know how dangerous fire is?" She fretted and fumed. "The arrogance! The gall! arrgh!" Then Amelia suddenly remembered her friends. "Oh, um, I'm sorry. I'm just sooo," she pursed her lips and burst out, "upset I could just … rrroohhh!" She rumbled and shook with frustration and anger.

"It's all right, little one." Felicity felt the little fairy's pain and anguish. Amelia looked so forlorn as she shuffled her feet with crossed arms. Her wings drooped and her head hung low. She looked like she was ready to cry. "Oh, you poor darling, come here." Felicity opened her arms, and Amelia rushed into them, sobbing. Tulip and Felicity comforted the distressed little fairy with soothing rubs and pats.

Felicity stroked Amelia's hair and rocked her back and forth. "Shush, shush, little one," she crooned. Felicity put her handless wrist under Amelia's chin and raised her head until they could see eye to eye. "Now listen to me and be brave. Opus and I are very old, so much more then we look because this is just the way we were carved. We have been up here all alone for far too many years to count." Then Felicity looked off dreamily. "For a while, I would pray that Opus and I would go to sleep like Grandpa did, so we, too, could be part of the dream in heaven. I thought it would be just grand to wake up to Grandpa, the children, Mother, and Father. We would be a family again." She giggled with a new thought. "Now our dreams will be full of loving fairies, laughing and playing with the whole family."

Amelia sniffled and scrunched her tear-stained face and runny nose into Felicity's side as she raised her puffy eyes adoringly.

Opus was awed. "Wow, Felicity, I didn't know you understood about Grandpa's passing. All these years, I thought you were just too naïve to know the truth. I've been trying to protect your feelings."

"Well, I have been playing along, keeping positive thoughts and trying to keep

Mr. Grumpy entertained. I balanced out your pessimism with my optimism." She smiled at him adoringly.

Opus thought she could not have looked more lovely as he reached down and squeezed her hand endearingly.

As Tulip heard more of the puppets' feelings, she became more and more concerned about the tone of their thoughts. By the end of their comments, she felt downright indignant! "It sounds like you're giving up!" She wagged her finger at Felicity like a scolding parent. "You're not allowed to go to sleep, pass away, burn up, or even stay here. You're in our family now, and we're going to do something about it. Right, Amelia?"

Amelia snuffled one last time, wiped her nose with Felicity's apron, and said with conviction, "Right!" She moved from Felicity and started to pace.

But when Opus started to argue, Amelia warned, "Shush! I'm thinking." Opus was taken aback by being ordered by one so young. He just stared at her wide-eyed with surprise.

Amelia paced back and forth as she pondered what to do. She paced so vigorously she wore a path in the dust. Every once in a while, one could see the spark of an idea go off in her head. Then she would whip her ponytails back and forth and shake the idea right out of her head because it was a bad idea. She flexed her wings and continued to fuel her brainstorming.

While Amelia was experiencing a scrambling of the brain, Tulip glanced down at her feet and saw Felicity's wooden hand on the floor. A sudden burst of inspiration came over her. "Hey, Amelia, let's ask Solomon."

"Shush," Amelia ordered.

"But," Tulip tried again.

"Quit chattering, Tulip. I'm thinking," Amelia snapped.

Before, Tulip was just frustrated by her best friend not listening to her. Now she was downright upset. She picked up the wooden hand and tossed it at Amelia. *Konk!* It biffed her on the back of the head.

"Ouch!" Amelia rubbed the back of her head and looked to see what hit her. She spotted the hand and picked it up. The new thought hit her too. "I've got it. We'll go see Solomon. He's so old and wise, he'll know what to do."

Good idea! Tulip generously replied.

Oblivious to what had happened and proud of herself, Amelia said, "Yeah, it is. Glad I thought of it."

Both Felicity and Tulip slapped hands to their foreheads with exasperation and groaned.

Amelia looked confused as she took all three into her gaze. "What?"

Felicity and Tulip looked at each other knowingly, and giggled. Opus was confused by the whole exchange. All he could think of was that girls were confusing, to say the least.

Amelia shrugged off the feeling that she was being mocked and took command with some urgency, quickly explaining her plan. "Look, I'm going to need to borrow this." She held up the hand so Felicity could see what she was taking. "I need to show it to Solomon, or he'll never believe me." She tucked the hand into a pouch and without a backward glance, took off out the broken window.

Tulip shook her head at her best friend's rudeness. "We'll be back before dark. I promise." Tulip crossed her heart. "And Berry Bear promises too." She crossed the bear's heart as well.

R. S. Rayborn

She gave Felicity a quick squeeze goodbye. She then rose up to Opus and gave him a peck on the cheek Suddenly, Tulip covered her mouth and blushed a deep red as she realized she had just kissed a boy. She tittered coyly, fluttered her eyes at Opus a couple of times, and then zoomed out after Amelia.

"What was that?" Opus asked, a little shocked and bewildered.

"Opus," Felicity reached up for his hand, "do you really believe they can help us?" she asked hopefully.

Opus answered, "They're going to try, Felicity. They're going to try."

CHAPTER 3
LITTLE LOST FAIRIES: THE FLIGHT HOME

While the puppets pondered the recent events, Tulip caught up with Amelia, who was hovering high in the sky. Amelia looked toward the morning sun and headed off just to the right of the glowing orb, which appeared to be sitting on top of the mountain.

As they flew, Tulip grumbled at Amelia. "I told you we flew too far, but nooohh, you had to follow those toady old trolls to their hole!"

Amelia was ignoring Tulip's tirade as she was nearly out of earshot and flying hard. After a long while of steady flight, Amelia landed atop a tall tree for a rest and a look-see. Tulip was winded when she landed. She looked back toward where they had come from and beheld a carpet of green treetops as far as the eye could see. "I hope they're still okay," she said, meaning the stranded puppets.

Amelia looked and was worried as she searched the area for something familiar.

Tulip saw the anxiety in her friend's eyes. "Are we lost?"

Amelia bit her lip and then softly started reciting an old nursery rhyme. Tulip recognized it from their early days in the nest, when Solomon would wiggle the baby fairies from one limb to another. He would sing out his rhymes, always catching the babies with his last word. The baby fairies, with their immature wings, would laugh and giggle. They would yell "Hooray!" and, "Let's do it again." This was how Solomon taught the babies not to fear flying. Tulip always thought that the silly little poems were only funny. I mean, really, who ever heard of a lost fairy? Now Tulip understood that the rhyme was a mental guide home. She was relieved that Amelia remembered it. She cupped an ear toward Amelia, who kept repeating the rhyme as she looked for familiar landmarks.

Little Lost Fairy

Little lost fairy, in the dark woods alone,
    You wandered off far from home. As she weeps on the cold damp loam.
    A warty old toad hopped up on his mushroom throne.
    He asked, "Why do you weep little one?"
    "I chased flutterbys for a whittle fun!"
    "Ah! And like a naughty little fairy who lost her way, you should have known better where to stay.
    If you wish to be safe and sound, heed my words so home can be found.
    Fly high in the sky when the new day is born.

Face the rising sun early in the morn. See the misty mountains that sparkle with dew.

To the right of the sun she flew. Once you find the Snaky River, Up you'll follow till a rumble makes you shiver.

Up, up the crying mountain you go to reach a plateau that nobody will know.

At the top, an ogre faces the way to a little brook, and the course you must stay.

Follow the little brook up the gully to your haven at Beaver Dam Valley. Now you are home, little lost fairy. Rejoice and be wary whenever you roam."

"I see it," Amelia said excitedly pointing off into the distance. Tulip shaded her eyes and could barely see the shimmering curves of Rattle Snake River. "We'll head that way to where the river meets the mountain."

Amelia took off at an easy pace, and Tulip followed. They flew to the river and followed its path upstream toward the mountain. The river turned into a gorge. When they rounded the last bluff, they were greeted by a mighty sound. It was the roar of a tower of water raining down. "Look, Tulip," Amelia yelled. "The mountain is crying."

"You think we have time for a bath?" Tulip yelled.

"Sure. A quick one," Amelia yelled back.

They went to the edge of the waterfall, where the water drops only sprinkled, and showered in the cold drizzle. By the time they were done, the sun had risen high enough for the fairies to dry on the warm rocks. Relaxed and warmed by the sun's rays, Amelia said, "We're going to have to remember this place and build a dwelling here."

"But the roar is way too loud. How could you ever sleep?" Tulip had to yell for Amelia to hear her.

Amelia shrugged. "You dried off enough to fly?"

"Yep!"

"Well then, up we go."

So the fairies rose to the top of the waterfall, where they saw a huge field of flowers of all colors next to the river. Following the river upstream until it forked, they saw a large boulder that looked like a sleeping ogre facing the river.

"We head up this brook," Amelia said. They followed the brook quite far, till it opened into a hidden glen that smelled of onions.

Tulip held her nose. "PU! Can we go now?"

"Yes, let's go." They launched themselves straight up and looked at the horizon to the right of the sun. There in the distance, the shadows were just leaving Beaver Dam Valley.

"Home again." Amelia smiled at Tulip. With her hands clasped under her chin, Tulip beamed at Amelia with a "my hero" look upon her face and fluttered her eyes. Amelia smiled back. She beckoned Tulip to follow and lifted off. She knew exactly where Solomon had sunk his roots and wanted to waste no time.

The brook skirted the glen to the lea side of the mountain. The beavers and fairies had built a very intricate and functional dam there. The resulting pool held rainbow trout and tadpoles to chase and play with. The fairies had set up a spillway for some of the water to feed their crops, and the rest of the water went to bathing and washing pools.

Below the dam, a tree-length from the shore, stood Solomon from where he kept watch over the valley. Solomon had rooted there because the earth was nutritious, and the ground was firm but moist. When the fairies spotted the mighty oak, they could see he had lost some of his smaller branches and many leaves from the storm. Much of the moss that had hung from his branches was littered on the ground. Yet, over all, he looked as formidable as ever. A grand old oak was he, 150 fairies tall. and branches that stretched out almost as wide. His lichen-covered limbs were like strong, heavy arms that hung low and wide of his trunk.

The fairies landed on a branch and gazed upon his sleeping face. He presented a wizened and relaxed visage. A deep rumbling and creaking sound came from him. Tulip giggled because he always made such funny snoring sounds when he slept.

Amelia shouted, "Hey, old thing, wake up!"

Solomon just kept snoring.

"Wake up!" Amelia shouted. She jumped up and down on the branch. He gave a little twitch of one limb, then scratched his trunk with another limb. The movement shook the whole tree till he settled back down and started snoring again. Amelia stood there on the branch, getting very irritated. Her arms were crossed, and she tapped her foot. With a fierce look, she said, "I'll wake him up." She launched herself at top speed, bouncing her feet against his forehead. "Waaake up!"

He snorted, brushed at his face with another branch, and again settled back down.

Amelia hovered with furious wing speed and fumed at the sleeping giant.

"Maybe I can help you," Tulip suggested.

With an impish grin, Amelia agreed. "Yeah, let's both knock on his forehead." Amelia circled back and looped around Tulip, picked up speed, and then zoomed forward and bounced against his forehead harder. As she recoiled, Tulip repeated Amelia's flight and bounced from his forehead too. They were giggling and bouncing, looping around the branch and bouncing again and again as in a fun game.

"Snot! Wha? What's this?" Solomon, at last waking, bellowed his annoyance in a deep baritone voice. He thrashed his limbs at his face, trying to shoo away whatever was plaguing him. Finally recognizing them, he grumbled, "Impish little feys, disrespecting their elders."

As his eyes began to focus, he saw his two favorite fairies on a branch in front of him. But after being so rudely awakened and spending the night fraught with worry, he was still beside himself with frustration. Tulip had landed and was sitting there without a care in the world, lazily swinging her legs back and forth. Amelia, standing next to her with arms crossed and a little too haughty an expression for her diminutive size, waited to speak.

Solomon let himself feel a moment of elation at seeing his younglings safe at home. He let that feeling melt away and then assumed a very stern and authoritative countenance. He towered there, his limbs akimbo and a root tapping. He looked just like an angry parent. "Oh, it's you two. And where have you been, young ladies? I've been worried sick!"

As the silence grew, a staring contest continued between Solomon and Amelia. They glared at each other with mutual disapproval and waited each other out.

Tulip giggled away at them. She was tickled pink with their behavior. This wasn't the first time they had this war of wills. They were acting like a couple of old crows, waiting to see which way the worm would turn and who would get to eat it. It was fun to watch and wonder who would crack first: Solomon, who turned redwood with frustration, or Amelia, who turned blue from holding her breath. It couldn't last much longer. Amelia made a silly face, and Solomon burst out laughing.

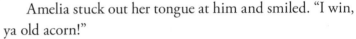

Amelia stuck out her tongue at him and smiled. "I win, ya old acorn!"

He pulled the branch the fairies were sitting on close to his face and gave them a whiskery hug. "You two are going to worry the bark right off me. That storm almost blew me off my roots." He moved his limb back into position and continued. "I could only imagine what that storm was doing to my little feys!"

Both of the young fairies looked sheepish, and sincerely said, "We're sorry."

"Well, I'm happy to see you home, safe and sound. And surprised to see you unhurt, clean, and well rested." Solomon squinted curiously at Tulip as he spoke. "You must have had a very good place to hide from the storm." Solomon let his words trail off as his attention was drawn to the animal Tulip was holding. "Tulip!"

She jumped and squealed, "Yes Solomon?"

"That is the smallest bear I have ever seen. Why isn't it moving?" he asked.

"Because it's a cuddly, stuffed with fluff and made by noisy giants. He was broken, so I fixed him," she explained.

Solomon was shocked. All the color had drained from his bark. He had been very worried about his lost little feys. Out of all the fledglings he had taught, these two mischievous little imps seemed to get into the most trouble. He loved them dearly, as if they were his own little saplings. In his current horrified state, he turned his anger on the leader of the duo. "And just what were you doing around noisy giants, young lady?"

Amelia instantly went into her excuse mode. "Well, you see, it was like this. We were working hard at our daily chores," she started. This Solomon interpreted they were off scaring flutterbys or getting into mischief. "Then we spied some, um, movement at the wild strawberry patch."

Aha, they were hungry and sneaking a snack, Solomon thought.

"It turned out to be a toady old troll, rooting around for free food. So we gave chase."

This meant they were outside the vale, sneaking away from their chores, Solomon thought.

"We were about to capture him at Spy-It-Rock." He knew they were outside the valley. "Then suddenly, the sky grew dark, and the wind reached out of the gray clouds and grabbed us."

As her story progressed, she became very animated. She wrapped both her arms around herself tightly. "We were blown and twisted all over the place." Amelia flew off his branch and spun and tumbled all about as if the storm had her in its clutches again.

Tulip giggled with delight. Amelia always made the best excuses.

Solomon just rolled his eyes. He was used to all of Amelia's tall tales and could read between the lines to know the true meaning of the exhausting verbiage. So he urged her to continue. "Hmmm, very interesting. Go on."

"Then the wind blew us a million miles away. And *whoosh*, we burst through the window of a noisy giant's dwelling and hit a back wall hard." Amelia demonstrated as she thudded into a branch and made it vibrate. She fell dramatically toward the ground. Luckily, she caught herself at the last moment, just before she went splat on the ground. Swiftly, she sprang up and continued her lurid tale. "It was dark, dusty, and really, really creepy." Amelia's recall became more farfetched and sensational. "The wind howled through the broken window, and we could hear bones rattling in the gloom. I bravely ventured into the dim room, when suddenly two vicious noisy giants pounced—"

"Amelia!" Tulip interrupted loudly. "Opus and Felicity are our friends."

"Oh, sorry." Amelia was sheepish. She realized she may have exaggerated her story a little. All right, all right, she exaggerated a lot.

"Well, Amelia?" Solomon prodded.

"Okay, okay. We were blown into a noisy giant's dwelling. And after scaring ourselves silly, we met some new friends. At first we thought they were noisy giants, but they were only this tall." She indicated the height by holding her hand over Tulip's head.

"Oh, really?" Solomon said skeptically.

"Yes, really. They looked just like noisy giants, only a lot smaller. And you know what else? They were made of wood!"

"Amelia," Solomon rebuked. "Now you have gone too far. Made of wood? My word! What will you come up with next?" he said in disbelief.

Tulip jumped to her friend's defense. "No, really, Solomon. They're tangled and tied to this box they call a theater. And they're weak and have a hard time moving their arms and legs. And even worse, the real noisy giants want to destroy our friends' home, and, and," Tulip burbled.

"Calm down, little one. You are not making any sense. We old-timers are a little slow, and it takes me a little while to think clearly and understand." Tulip's outburst caused Solomon to believe there might be some truth to Amelia's story. "Now, more slowly, what's this all about?"

Amelia took a deep breath to calm herself. Then she continued her tale without the fantasy. "We were blown into the top room of a noisy giant's dwelling and found these wooden people with strings attached hanging in this box."

"Go on," he urged.

"Their names are Opus and Felicity. They are twice as big as me and tell the most wonderful stories. And they sing and dance. They called themselves puppets." Amelia had a confused look on her face for a moment and then asked Tulip, "What was that other word they used to describe what they were?"

"Marionette," Tulip responded. "Marionettes or puppets."

"They're our friends. They're in danger, and yes, they are made of wood. See!" Amelia held up the hand so Solomon could see it.

He moved his branch closer to get a better look. He was surprised to see the wood grain in the hand. He also saw how delicate and lifelike it looked. "It's made from a tree!" he exclaimed. "Yet I sense something more. Let me smell it, Amelia."

"Okay, just let me get braced first." Amelia wrapped her legs and one arm around a branch and then held the hand under Solomon's huge nose-like burl. "Okay, smell."

Solomon inhaled deeply. Amelia held the hand tightly, so it wouldn't get sucked up the opening in the burl.

Tulip had flitted out of the way. She had learned from a bad past encounter what it's like to be sucked up an oak tree's nose. Luckily, it was only twenty years old and a mere stripling. Tulip was stuck rump-first up its nose for two days. The young tree had a runny nose, and it took days for Tulip to get all the sap off after she escaped. She certainly didn't want a repeat of that experience, so she stayed out of the way.

Solomon finished sniffing the hand and was surprised. As he moved his branch back into position, he said, "Well, bless my acorns! I know that tree. That's old Elmer. We used to call him Stumpy, until he was broken and blown over. He lingered for a long time, but life eventually ebbed out of him. I felt a terrible loss. We were friends from the time we were just sprouts. Now those pesky skyads have taken up residence in his stump and branches. But that was a long, long time ago.

R. S. Rayborn

I don't understand how a piece of him could still have the scent and vibes of life after so long."

Tulip flew over and gave his cheek a hug. "We're sorry for your loss, great-grandfather tree."

Solomon stirred out of his sorrowful reminiscence and smiled. "It happened a long time ago, Tulip, and it is part of the cycle of life in nature. So you say these puppets, these friends of yours, are made of Elmer?"

Amelia flitted up and stood on the tip of Solomon's nose. "Yes, I guess. If you say the hand has Elmer's scent. The story we heard was that the puppets' family's grandfather carved them from a branch he collected."

Solomon tried to look at her and went all cross-eyed. "Leave off, youngling. You're making me dizzy!" The two little fairies fluttered back to his branch. "That's better. Then it seems, somehow, Stumpy is living on through a created progeny," he pondered.

"But we have to hurry," Tulip offered anxiously. "Those noisy giants we saw said they were going to burn the dwelling down tonight. Our friends are still in it and will be lost forever!"

"What?" Solomon became indignant. All trees understood the danger of fire. "Tell me the story again. From the beginning." Solomon listened intently as the fairies took turns in relating the events that had happened, the new friends they had made, and all the things they saw, right up to the moment they arrived home.

"Hmmmm, this is very serious. I need a moment to think." He pondered all they had told him. He was in awe at how strong Elmer's apparent will to live was. "I must speak with your seneschal and healers. I believe that with some of Stumpy's sawdust and their wisdom, we may be able to heal your friends' weaknesses. Please go and tell her all you have told me. And Amelia, no tall tales! I'm sure Julia is tired of your antics too," he warned.

"Okay, we'll be right back," Amelia said, and they flew away up the brook.

They flew to the sunny side of the southern mountain. The morning mist was still burning off. Already, fey folk were working in the fields. At the foot of the mountain, tucked into the foliage, was a stone fair dwelling. Next to the dwelling was a beautiful and aromatic herb garden. At the back of the garden, a large arbor of grapes provided shade for the seneschal, Julia, and her retinue.

The two fairies landed outside the arbor entrance and respectfully approached their seneschal on foot.

Julia sat on her flower throne, studying a leaf report. Dixie, Julia's assigned protector, leaned on her spear, and with a lazy, bored expression, looked at the report over Julia's shoulder.

A twig snapped as Amelia and Tulip approached. Instantly, Dixie pounced into action. She leaped in front of Julia, spear at the ready, to protect her. "Halt, ya little maggots!" Her adrenaline was pumping, since she knew well these two little pranksters, though secretly, she was pleased that they were breaking up her boredom. Because of Amelia's impish nature, Dixie took every opportunity she could to make the little imp squirm. "What are you two troublemakers doing here? If you have no appointment, you have no business here, so scat," Dixie barked.

Amelia placed her hands on her hips and sassed back, "I'm here 'cause it's nunya!"

"Nunya? What's that mean" Dixie asked, confused.

"Nunya business! We're here to see Mother Julia, you dried-up old prune," Amelia retorted.

"Troll," Dixie spat back.

"Toad," Amelia retaliated.

"Scaredy frog," Tulip joined in.

"Why you pugnacious little warts. I'll," Dixie said as she advanced toward them.

"Dixie," Julia said, her eyes not leaving the report. "Remember what I said about catching more flies with honey?"

"Yes, chief," Dixie acknowledged a little shortly as she kept her eyes on the intruders. Amelia stuck her tongue out at the ill-tempered protector fairy. "Did you see that?" huffed Dixie. After a moment of total silence, and seeing the sudden ill-look on Amelia's and Tulip's faces, Dixie turned to see Julia, sternly peering over the top of the leaf report. Dixie cringed sheepishly, faced Julia, and bowed in contrition. "Yes, mistress," she said as she took her place next to Julia at parade rest.

The girls knew that look as well. Their faces paled as they knelt to the ground.

Amelia knew they were in trouble and did the only correct thing she thought appropriate at the time. She prostrated herself to make her really small and humble. Tulip was feeling ashamed and started to sniffle.

Though Julia had looked like she was reading her report, she actually had watched the little melodrama unfold. She was also angry that it was these two rascals again. The only reason she didn't pack them off to protector fairy school was because she saw something special in her pixilated foundlings. Julia just wished she could get through to their generation about responsibility. Surprised, Julia spotted Berry Bear and pointed. "What is that?" she asked.

Tulip sat up and wiped her nose on the back of her arm. She held Berry out toward Julia so she could see him better. "It's my new cuddly, see? His name is Berry Bear."

Julia forgot about the scolding she had started to give them and arose from her flower chair. "May I see him?" she asked Tulip, reaching for her stuffy.

"Sure." Tulip passed the bear into Julia's hands.

Julia examined Berry. Fine cloth was rare to the fairies. In that regard, Berry was a treasure. She marveled at Tulip's fine stitching and the thread and fabric used. The fairies regularly made fine things from nature, but noisy giant things seemed to last longer, and they made for softer nests.

"We also have this to show you and a message from Solomon." Amelia gave Julia the wooden hand.

Julia compared the hand to hers. It was as delicate as her own yet made of wood.

"What have you scamps been up, to and where did this come from?" Julia looked down at her little subjects, perplexed.

Amelia launched into a briefer version of their overnight adventure with only a few minor corrections by Tulip. Amelia spoke the truth from the time they ditched their chores to the meeting with Solomon and his sad, sad tale about Elmer.

"Well, it seems there's no end to your misadventures." Julia took a deep breath and hummed to herself in thought. "As for your new friends, I see the love you have for them. I also see from your cuddly, Tulip," she handed Berry Bear back to her and Tulip hugged him tightly, "that there may be much value the clan can salvage before the dwelling is destroyed." Julia walked back to her seat, turned. And faced all who were in attendance. "We are one with the forest and trees, and as your new friends are their kin, I declare that this clan will help them."

Amelia and Tulip hugged each other and danced with joy.

"Dixie!" Julia turned to her protector fairy. "Take Amelia and ask the sages to meet me at Solomon's. Oh, and make sure you root Prunella out of her cubby. She needs to be out and enjoy some fresh air anyway."

"But, but I'm your protector, not some babysitter or go-for," she whined indignantly. "I need to stay with you!"

Julia put a hand up to stop the protest, and Dixie was silent. "I'm giving you an important mission. After you get the sages, I want you and Amelia to go to the skyads and retrieve some of Elmer's sawdust."

"Great! I'll call up five squads of protectors. We'll come at them from all sides, we'll—"

"No!" Julia commanded.

"What?" Dixie asked, looking confused.

"I want just you and Amelia to go."

"Huh? No way, not her," Dixie ranted. That layabout spends more time day-dreaming than working. Why I've caught them in the pollen bin, swelling themselves silly. I've seen them—"

"Enough," Julia interrupted. "We're not trying to start a war, Dixie. Listen to me. When the need arises, I want you to defer to Amelia's wisdom. She has been teasing and fooling the scrubby skyads ever since she could fly and knows them well." Amelia turned red with embarrassment. "She may even surprise you, given the chance." Julia smiled and nodded once at Amelia.

Amelia curtsied to Julia but stuck her tongue out at Dixie and gave her the ninner-ninner dance when Julia had turned away.

"Are those my troops?" Dixie pointed at Amelia.

"Yes," Julia said as she turned to Amelia. Amelia looked angelic, but Julia knew better. "Remember, Amelia, Dixie's in charge!"

Dixie stuck her tongue out at Amelia, giving her back a ninner-ninner face. Then she walked over and put her hand on top of Amelia's head, tousling her hair. Amelia pushed Dixie's hand off grumpily and frowned.

"Oh, chief, what if Prunella won't budge? You know how she gets about her studies," asked Dixie.

"Just tell her that I'm going to a noisy giant's dwelling, and you won't be able to stop her." Dixie smiled at Julia and then snapped a crisp salute. Amelia watched

Dixie a bit subdued and copied her salute. "Oh, when you retrieve the sawdust, take it directly to Solomon. He will tell you what to do next."

Tulip jumped up and stood next to her playmate. "Okay, let's get going!"

"You're not going with them, Tulip," Julia replied.

"Why not?" Tulip suddenly looked really worried. She grabbed Amelia's hand fiercely and squeezed her bear tightly. She didn't like the idea of being separated from her best friend.

Julia went to Tulip and caressed her face. "You, Tulip, will be my special helper. You need to show us the way to your friends' dwelling and make introductions."

"That's great, Tulip. You have your own mission." Amelia gave her a big hug. "Tell Opus and Felicity we'll be there real soon."

"Come on, little soldier," Dixie called. "It's time to go."

Julia bade them safe journey and fair winds. Amelia squeezed Tulip's hand and followed Dixie out.

Tulip stood there near tears, and Julia rested a hand on her shoulder. As Tulip waved goodbye to her friend, she sniffled again, and a tear rolled down her cheek. Julia gave her a comforting hug and smiled down at her young charge. The tears made Tulip look vary waiflike and forlorn.

Julia lifted Tulip's chin till the little fey faced her and said soothingly, "Tears shed over the love of your friend are healing and good. You will see them soon enough. little flutterby. Now let me look at you." Julia wiped Tulip's face clean and made her honk her nose into a handkerchief. "Much better. Let's see, what shall we do with Mr. Berry Bear while we're away?"

Tulip tightened her grip on her stuffy. Having just lost her best friend and now to leave behind her protector bear was just too much! "Berry doesn't wanna be left behind," she sobbed.

Julia was aware of Tulip's attachment and her need for security, but she also knew Tulip would be very busy and need her hands free. The warmhearted leader had an idea and suggested, "Dear, all of my workers will be much too busy to watch over my throne room. Would Berry do me a big favor and guard my throne while we are away?"

Tulip held Berry to her ear and a look of surprise crossed her face. "He says he would be honored to be your guard here."

R. S. Rayborn

"Good! Let's see, have him sit on my throne. That should scare any intruders off." Julia urged Tulip toward the throne.

Tulip smiled, turned, and skipped over to the throne. She placed Berry on the seat with one arm on the armrest. "Guard well," she told Berry, "and I'll see you soon. Then she kissed the bear on the nose and stepped back.

"Wait, he's not ready yet." Julia walked over and put a garland of forget-me–not's at a jaunty angle upon his head and a wooden scepter across his lap to complete the image. "There, now he is our palace Bugbear and will instill fear in all who tread near." Tulip beamed with pride at Berry, but he just sat there, stoic and regal looking.

Julia ruffled Tulip's hair. "Come, let's go see Solomon." Away they flew out of the trellised court. As they flew over the fields, Julia sent word out with the sprites that all fey folk were to gather at Solomon's.

When Julia arrived, she settled upon the branch facing Solomon, and Tulip landed at her side. Julia curtsied before Solomon regally and then smiled as she addressed him. "You weathered the storm well, grand old oak."

While Julia was addressing Solomon, fey folk of all kinds were gathering in Solomon's boughs, at his roots, and in the surrounding area. The tiny and mischievous white-socks pixies flitted in and about. They could be quite annoying because they were as small as a bumblebee and just as fast. Brownies and fauns showed up from their work in the fields and trees.

Solomon returned the smile. "Ahh, my little sapling. It's been too long. You grow more beautiful each time I see you."

Julia blushed and acted coy. "Cavalier as ever, you old smoothie," she flirted.

"And if I keep shedding my bark, I will be smooth." He guffawed at his own joke. "I do feel my age, though. I have such a creak in my trunk." He placed large limbs behind his trunk and stretched. The fairies heard loud groans and pops of his wooden frame as he straightened out. "My old branches are getting stiffer and stiffer. I think my time for the long sleep comes to me soon."

"Not you, old soul. You are still as strong as a mountain and will last as long," she cajoled.

"Thank you, my dear one. But time runs short, and we have much to do before darkness falls. I'm assuming Amelia and Tulip have apprised you of the situation."

"Yes, they have," she answered. "The callousness of the noisy giants is terrible! Their disregard for Mother Earth, and even their own kind, is disheartening. It seems impossible to find one with a pure heart."

"Let's make our plans quickly then," Solomon urged.

"I have already sent for the healers. Ah, see, they're flying in now. I have also dispatched Dixie and Amelia to retrieve some of Elmer's sawdust."

"Excellent. Amelia knows the scrubby skyad's habits and has the best chance to succeed. We need the essence of Elmer for the healing tincture," he explained.

Julia nodded and said, "I've ordered Prunella to be prepared and available. Here she is."

Prunella stood tall and gangly. She was older than Julia, though she didn't look it. You could consider her pretty if you cared for that sort of thing. Her hair was an unruly mop, usually held together with two or three quills stuck in a twist of tresses. She wore oversized round spectacles, so she could read the many books and scrolls in her library. Her dress was a simple beige wraparound tunic with green trim and a cloud-blue shawl thrown over here shoulders. Still, she was the wisest sage in the clan. She had a no-nonsense attitude when she went-a-doctoring, and she always seemed to find a cure. She was a naturalist with a heavy interest in noisy giants. She didn't like her studies being interrupted by trivial or the mundane, but this adventure had certainly spiked her interest.

"We'll be going soon enough. Let me tell you what is going on and what we need." Julia outlined the problem and the general plan. Then she finished with, "We will bring them back here for the final healing. Afterwards, you can inspect the noisy giant artifacts to your heart's content."

Giddy with the anticipation of a fledgling, Prunella started bouncing up and down. "What are we waiting for then? Let's go!"

"First, I need to designate duties. I would like you to choose four more healers to come with us, and give the rest their orders in preparing the remedy." Julia then turned to the assembly and announced, "I need the protector fairies and strong workers to follow me. The ground fey and fledglings will stay behind and follow the orders of Solomon and the sages." Julia turned to Solomon. "Send Dixie and Amelia on as soon as the remedy is prepared."

"It will be ready," Solomon assured her.

Julia placed her hand on Tulip's shoulder and smiled at her. "My little moppet, you lead the way." Tulip nodded and took to the sky, with Julia and Prunella close behind. Almost all of the fairies took flight and followed their seneschal. The rest dispersed to their designated tasks, gathering the rest of the needed ingredients and preparing for the ritual of the ingredient.

Solomon waved his branches goodbye and bade them, "Fair winds, my lovelies."

CHAPTER 4
THE SCRUBBY SKYADS

The sun was past the zenith when Amelia and Dixie landed next to a boulder. Stealthily, Amelia peeked around the rock at the remnants of Elmer in the distance. There was a clearing around the stump, and a fairy ring of toadstools encircled it.

Blackberry brambles had become thickly interlaced throughout Elmer's dead trunk and branches, making visibility very poor.

When Dixie looked around, she saw no movement, so she stood up and started forward passing Amelia. Amelia grabbed Dixie's belt and jerked her back hard. "Wait," she whispered, "I think they know we're here." She gazed into the blackberries.

"How can you tell?" Dixie asked, turning back to Amelia and scanning the area very carefully.

"Because there is nothing moving," Amelia said softly.

Dixie looked around and finally registered the lack of sound. No insects chirped, no birds sang or flew over, and even the grass and wind were still.

Amelia held Dixie by the arm and locked eyes with her. "Listen, I've been sneaking around these tree fleas ever since I learned how to sneak away. They are stealthy, very strong, and can blend into almost any surrounding. When we do speak to them, you have to appeal to their distasteful natures. Show strength through intelligence. Insult them. Flatter them by telling them how horrible they are. You see, we'll play to their vanities and appetites." As she turned to go, she had another thought and turned back. "Maybe you better let me do all the talking. Oh, and leave the spear. It won't do you any good anyway." Amelia turned, and in a crouch, she moved away.

Dixie shook her hair and harrumphed. She crouched low and followed after her little ward.

Amelia headed toward the top of the fallen tree. She went to one knee at the edge of the blackberry briars and looked around. No alarms had been raised, so having chosen her path, she picked her way into the thicket. They made their way through the brush slowly and quietly. Thorns and twigs poked them and pulled at their clothing. Amelia paused for a moment and sniffed the air. She turned, and with a concerned look, whispered, "Whatever you do, don't fight back." She then moved forward again.

Dixie looked worried as the thicket closed in about her. She felt tiny tugs and scratches as she progressed though the bramble. Her left ankle seemed snagged on something, and in a loud whisper said, "Wait, I'm stuck!"

Amelia stopped and cringed at Dixie's words. She stood up, looked back, and in a clear voice said, "You're not stuck. We're caught."

Suddenly, twigs and limbs wrapped around the two fairies. "Gotcha," said a gruff voice.

Amelia was seized by a nasty-looking skyad. She was repulsed by his foul-smelling breath. "Whew," she said, turning her face away. You need to eat some spearmint!"

Outraged, he said, "Why you, I should pull your scrawny wings off right now, you little imp! Arrh! You're lucky I have orders to leave that pleasure to the exalted grand pooh bah." He was so angry he was slavering all down his chin like a rabid animal. His breath stank of rotted sugar plums. "Oooh, I could just squeeze you till your eyes pop out!"

"*Eeeh ooooomph!*" Amelia wheezed as the air was squeezed out of her.

Dixie yelled, "Leave her alone, ya big bully." The skyad squeezed tighter, and Amelia started to turn blue. Dixie thought quickly and asked, "What do you think his grand pooh bahness will do if you pop her now?"

Fear showed on the skyad's face, and he loosened his grip. Amelia coughed and sputtered, trying to regain her breath. He glared at Dixie and said, "That's just fine. While you slave away for us, I will have the privilege of whipping you with thorny vines. It will be my reward for capturing you."

"Ha! Carry me to your leader, you overgrown gobsnot. And be quick about it," Amelia ordered. Dixie and the gruff skyad just stared in surprise at the young fairy's audacity.

Amelia's captor held her up to get a better look at her and reassess his prize. He thought, *Who does this little puffball think she is?* Then he worried, *Maybe the pooh bah has plans for her I don't know about!*

"Come on! Chop-chop!" Amelia barked.

This broke her captor's train of thought. He put on his meanest mug, brought her up real close, and said, "Be careful what you ask for!" Then he exhaled his stinky breath in her face.

"Blech, gag!" she coughed. He tucked her under his limbs, feet forward, head backward, and set out toward the stump. As the gruff skyad pushed his way through the briar, thin branches and vines spanked Amelia on the rump.

"Ow, yeawtch! Watch it, you repugnant stooge! Ouch!" The skyad smiled as they weaved their way through to the broken end of the tree trunk.

From her vantage point, Amelia could see that four skyads carried a struggling Dixie. Dixie could see Amelia too and glared disgustedly at her. Amelia just smiled and gave her a confident two thumbs up.

When they cleared the brambles at the end of the trunk, the gruff skyad held his captive aloft. From the scrub brush and briar, hundreds of skyads appeared.

Dixie's eyes grew wide with surprise at seeing such a multitude.

As they moved forward, they heard a tirades of sneers and taunts. "Hiss!" "Rake 'em over the coals!"" Boo!" "Pin their ears back!" "Revolting!" "They smell clean!" "Roast 'em raw!" With knotted brows they scowled and sneered. The fairies could hear the skyads' menace in their hearts.

In the center of the fairy ring of toadstools stood the remnants of Elmer's old stump. Broken and rent down its center, time and termites had created a hollow in its middle. In front of the stump grew a large red toadstool. The fairies were dropped a few paces in front of the mushroom.

Dixie immediately jumped up, ready to fight. This only made the general mob sneer and laugh more. They rattled and pounded their sharp crooked spears at her. "Are you ready to fight, Amelia?" When Dixie heard no answer, she looked over her shoulder and saw Amelia, sitting on her feet, abasing herself.

"Face the dirt, you worm!" a ruthless skyad growled as he prodded Dixie with his spear.

"Amelia?" Dixie looked at her questioningly.

"Would you get down here? You're embarrassing me," Amelia urged.

Unsure, Dixie went down on her knees next to the large mushroom. The herald pounded his gnarled staff three times, and all went silent.

In a loud, ancient, high-pitched voice, he heralded, "Presenting his exalted, lofty, grandiose, officially reprehensible, malodorous, the ultimate plutocrat. He' so big, he's gargantuan. The gruesome, all-authority, your august leader, Grand Pooh Bah Poison Sumac! All hail and tremble in your roots!"

The enthusiastic cheer from the horde was deafening! Out of the darkened stump lumbered a squat, corpulent, and the most grotesque-looking skyad the fairies had ever seen. He was bloated beyond belief. His bark was flakey, and he oozed sap from cracks in his wood. His head and neck were so large they seemed part of his trunk. The most ordinary thing about him was the old soup can lodged on top of his head as his crown. He stood in front of the large toadstool and waved his chubby gnarled limbs at his subjects.

Dixie was fascinated, as well as grossed out. When she felt a tug on her arm, she looked down to see Amelia, who was indicating that Dixie should be bowing down just like she was. Dixie did bow, but could not stop staring at the skyad king.

The riotous tumult from the crowd continued as Poison Sumac lowered his stout frame onto the large mushroom. It strained under his weight.

The herald pounded his staff, and all went silent again. With his shining red eyes, Sumac spotted Amelia. A sneering smile creased his shaggy, barked face. In a booming voice he exclaimed, "Aha, so I have caught you again, you vile little passion fairy. You have stolen my blackberries for the last time." He looked over the expansive rabble and asked them, "What shall we do with them, my scrubbies? Pull their wings off? Or just tie heavy stones to their ankles so they can't fly away?" The mob went wild over his cruel suggestions. "You!" He pointed his scepter at the fairies. A fat termite ran out from under his bark, down his stubby limb, to the end of the scepter. "You will be my personal servants." The termite stuck out his tongue and blew them a raspberry.

The crowd jeered with approval.

Amelia calmly sat up and folded her hands on her lap.

Dixie did the same. Speaking above the din, Amelia said, "Oh, great rotund one, your hideousness is truly frightful. We are totally nauseated."

At a gesture from his pooh bahness, all went silent. "Why, thank you," he answered.

"I have seen my sisters faint dead away at the mere utterance of your contemptible name," Amelia flattered.

"Really?" He puffed up with pride.

"Yes. Babies run screaming when tales of your slimy exploits are told. And the elders scratch themselves raw just at the thought of your royal itchiness," Amelia declared.

The mob whooped and cackled at the wonderful fear their leader instilled in the fairy populace.

Amelia again spoke loudly over the din. "We have come to swear loyalty to his rotundness." This evoked shocked rumbling from the masses.

"What?" Still sitting, Dixie, bolted to attention. "What are you getting us into? You're nothing but a, mmmph."

Amelia jumped up, put Dixie in a headlock, and covered her mouth. To the Sumac she said, "Yes, yes, a very obedient servant." She then whispered to the struggling protector fairy, "Knock it off, or you're going to get us in trouble." Dixie stopped struggling and was confused.

Amelia continued her deception. "Please forgive her outburst. She's just so happy to be here." To Dixie she whispered, "Just follow my lead." Then Amelia let go of her.

The mob had burst out riotously, thinking the fairies were wrestling. When Amelia let go, they indicated their disappointment with a round of boos and hisses.

The massive king eyed Amelia warily. He waved his hand, and the herald pounded the assembly to order. The grand pooh bah stroked his chin in a contemplative manner. "And what are the names of these potential citizens?"

"I'm Ratty Wormwook, and this is Miss Stinkweed." Amelia lied matter-of-factly.

"My but you have beautiful names. Musical and pleasant to the ear. What made you leave your tribe?"

Amelia smiled at Dixie for a moment. She knew she had the king hooked on her fairy tale. When she turned back to the pooh bah, she looked all meek and innocent. "Why? Because our seneschal mistreats us!"

"Oh? And just how does a loving passion fairy mistreat her subjects?"

Amelia took a couple of steps forward to better express herself to this lumbering lummox. "She would punish us in the foulest of ways, your drooling sappiness. Instead of spanking us, she would give us hugs."

"How grisly!" He cringed.

"When we're sick, she strokes our foreheads and feeds us dewdrop soup."

"Most awful."

"I know. Then she encourages us and nurtures us daily."

"You poor thing. No whips? No chains? Tell me more," he urged, showing great interest.

Amelia was very animated as she paced around and recited her yarn. All eyes were following her as she captivated her audience. Dixie sat in awe, her mouth agape, as she, too, was mesmerized by the web Amelia was weaving.

"Yet it was all a trick," Amelia expounded. "Our seneschal is really stingy. She keeps all the nectar and pollen for herself!"

"Nectar?" The pooh bah perked up at the mention of that precious, delectable substance.

"Yes! All she would feed us were brussels sprouts and lima beans, Yuck. She told us after that how much she loved us, while behind our backs, she was hoarding all that sweet honey for herself. Well, that was the last straw! That's when we decided to join your kingdom. You know how frail and helpless we fairies are. We need someone big and strong to protect us." Amelia turned to Dixie and winked.

His pooh bahness put a hand up to stall her delicious tale and sat back, placing one finger across his mouth in thought. He then smiled his sneering smile and asked, "And just what makes you think I would have you?"

"Um," Amelia faltered for a moment. She turned to Dixie, looked guilty, and shrugged. She mouthed silently to Dixie, *I'm sorry*. She was worried over the decision she had just made. She turned back to the grand pooh bah and said, "I know where the royal jelly is hidden!"

"No!" Dixie burst to her feet. Three skyads held their wicked spears menacingly on her.

"Quiet, you,' Sumac bellowed at Dixie. He then pointed a finger to the ground. One of the guards nodded and hit Dixie behind the knees. Dixie fell to the ground. She was angry but seethed silently.

Amelia looked so guilty, yet she had to continue her ruse. "I followed a line of bees from the seneschal's royal house far into the woods. You see, our seneschal doesn't trust us."

The pooh bah leaned forward. "That is the first sensible thing I've heard her do. I wouldn't trust my tribe with my bark shedding," he whispered to her. His herald, who overheard, just rolled his eyes.

Winking conspiratorially to him, Amelia raised her voice so all could hear. "I followed the bees to the hiding place. You could smell the honey from far off as you approached." The crowd of skyads slowly moved in rapt attention. "When I got there, the vault was so full, honey was oozing out of all the cracks and crevices."

The assembled mob leaned forward and licked their chops at the thought of the delicious royal jelly.

The skyads made the best blackberry and sugar plum wines, which is why they had such bad breath; they drank it all the time. But it was a rare treat for them to make honey mead. Royal jelly was ambrosia to them. "Well," the pooh bah urged Amelia to continue, "where is it?"

Flippantly, Amelia indicated, "Over that way, four or five valleys high up in a tree."

"But that's in the opposite direction of the fairy territories," he growled.

"Yes, exactly! I'm glad you appreciate the beauty of her deception."

"Huh? "You better not be tricking me!" He shook his scepter at her, and the termite on the end just harrumphed and tsk-tsked at her.

"Don't you see? By storing the honey on the other side of your kingdom, the rest of my clan wouldn't dare go there because they're afraid of you, oh, monstrous one."

"Fiendish! Ingenious! Your seneschal has a truly malevolent nature. I salute her!" He stood erect and placed his pudgy right hand and scepter over his heart (if he has a heart). "Besides, it shows just how stupid and weak you fairies are. Not being able to find a treasure like that left out in the open. Ha!"

"You're right. She feels it's so safe where it is she didn't even leave any protector fairies to guard it. Mind you, she doesn't trust the guards, either." Amelia added.

The pooh bah's eyes went wide with the knowledge of this fortuitous news. The horde teemed with excitement as well.

Amelia moved to stand closer to the pooh bah and faced the crowed. She made an opening gesture with her hands in front of his face, like opening a curtain. "Just imagine, high up in this tree is a great big honey hive. Oooozing its golden nectar. Dripping, drip, drip, drip. A huge, shining, golden dollop, dangling and glistening in the sun. The drops forming a delicious amber pool. The aroma of that ambrosia wafting through the air." As their bellies rumbled, the entire mob heaved a collective big sigh.

Breaking the hypnotic spell, Amelia became all matter-of-fact and said, "This, of course, drew some woodland creatures to sup from the pool."

"What?" Poison Sumac sputtered and coughed. He became indignant and said, "They're stealing my honey!"

"Yes," Amelia cried out. And with gusto she said, "I'm hungry! And those rotten little woodland creatures are eating all our honey!" She jumped up and down, thrusting her fists into the air. "Let's go save it!"

She ran full tilt into the mob. She yelled and screamed like a banshee. Turning, she excited the skyads as she passed them. This started a stampede, and the riotous mob pushed and shoved each other as they deserted the toadstool ring. The horde overtook and passed the little fairy. Amelia could hear the breathless ranting of the gluttonous tyrant as he approached from behind.

He yelled at his mutinous subjects, "Wait, wait for me! I am your pooh bah! Halt! I'm supposed to be first, darn it! Somebody needs to carry me." The sound of his voice diminished as he bounded away. Amelia slowed to a stop, out of breath. As the dust settled, she spied Sumac's scepter on the ground. *He must have dropped it when he passed me.* She picked it up and saw at the top of the

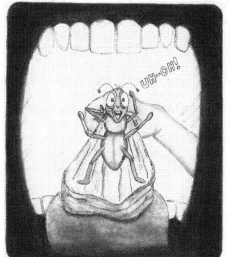

scepter, coughing and sputtering, clung the toady little termite. When the termite saw her smiling at him, he exclaimed in his tiny voice, "Uh oh," just before Amelia gulped him down.

After her little snack, she tossed the scepter over her shoulder and flew back to Dixie.

Dixie was still sitting on her feet, amazed at what she had witnessed. She was covered in dust, and the only word Dixie uttered to Amelia was, "Amazing!"

With a mild flip of her hand, Amelia said, "It was nothing."

"So Amelia," Dixie began as she rose and dusted herself off, "just where did you send them?"

"To a big old hornet's nest. It should take them all day to get there. Do you think the hornets will mind the invasion?"

Dixie chortled at the idea of the skyads running from the angry hornets. Feeling elated, the fairies flew over to the stump and filled their bags with sawdust. On their way home, Dixie retrieved her spear, and they flew with their heavy burden back to Solomon.

On arrival, they smelled the sweet scent of the brewing tonic simmering in the huge cooking pots. They dropped their bags of sawdust next to the cauldrons and went over to greet Solomon.

"Well?" Solomon asked. "How are those itchy little creatures?"

"Running to get the royal jelly from a hornet's nest."

"But hornets don't make honey," Solomon stated.

"I know that, and you know that, and soon the skyads will know that," she said slyly with a smile.

"You little imps." He laughed uproariously.

Dixie praised Amelia's accomplishments to Solomon. "You should have seen her, Solomon. She was unbelievable! I never dreamed her tall tales would come in so handy. You would think she was part wayward fairy the way she twisted them around her little finger. She was absolutely mesmerizing."

"You two have done well. But Julia is waiting for you to bring the tonic as quickly as possible. It is over there, in those flasks." Solomon pointed to a couple of drinking gourds cooling in the shade.

The young fairies picked up the flasks and draped the straps over their shoulders. Solomon bade them goodbye. "Off with you, and may you have fair winds to guide you." And away they flew toward the sinking sun.

CHAPTER 5
Lost Hope

After Tulip and Amelia left, the puppets started making plans. They talked about what kind of plays they would perform for the fairies, and wondered what their new home would be like. Would they be safe? Would there be dangerous animals about that might eat them? They were filled with excitement.

But the sun sank low on the horizon, and their little friends still had not returned. Hope was waning. And with the loss of hope went much of their remaining life force.

Much later that afternoon, the sounds of the arriving workmen caused panic to surge through Opus and Felicity. Tied to the theater box and not able to see what was happening outside, their imaginations ran wild. They heard clattering noises, and the sounds of the workmen hammering and milling below them were loud and frightening.

Suddenly, a generator roared to life, and the noise of breaking glass and hammers pounding away on the first floor reached them.

Felicity shook with fear as she lay crumpled on the floor of the theater. She sat up and whimpered. Then she curled into a ball and rocked back and forth.

Opus reached down to comfort her but was restrained by the strings. By sheer will, he forced his own frustrations and fears away.

"Felicity," he murmured gently. She continued to whimper and rock. A little louder he spoke her name again, "Felicity!" She stopped rocking and looked up at him, the strain of waiting plainly on her face. More soothingly he said, "The sun is still up, and there is plenty of time for those two little angels to come back."

"Do you really think so?" A small ray of hope appeared in Felicity's eyes.

He smiled with ease in his heart. "Yes, I really do." Then with encouragement, he said, "We don't have to sit here like a couple of frogs on a log. Look, your strings aren't hung up anymore. Maybe you can go around back and unhook me."

"But Opus, what if the girls don't come back?"

"Then we will just have to find a way to save ourselves. Come on, get up." Opus beckoned to her to take his hand. She took it hesitantly, and he helped her to her

R. S. Rayborn

feet. She felt weak and stood there, testing her balance. "Will you be able to walk?" he asked.

"Yes, I think so." She took some unsteady steps. Then she gathered her strings in her handless arm and stepped clumsily off the stage. Felicity looked around a little and felt a weird sense of freedom as she walked around the corner of the theater box. When she reached the farthest back corner, she was stopped by her strings. "I'm stuck!" she called loudly.

"Your controller paddles are hung up on the corner of the stage. Come back out front and pull them free."

She reappeared in front and pulled her strings tight. She jerked and tugged until the controllers came free.

Opus instructed, "Now pull your strings wide of the corners, and tell me what you see when you get back there."

She did as directed and pulled herself to the back. Felicity stood right under his controllers, and stretched up on her tippy-toes, "I can't reach them," she yelled.

"Find some boxes, blocks, anything to climb on. You're going to have to be high enough to push my controllers over the top," he called.

"Okay. Just a minute."

Opus only heard shuffling noises for a while. He was really frustrated at being so helpless. Then he heard a high-pitched squeak, squeak sound. "What's that noise?"

"I found a toy ark, with wheels. Ugh! I see why the children would get so exhausted after playing with us. It's tiring lugging the string and controllers around."

"Thank goodness the ark has wheels," Opus encouraged.

"Yeah, but it's still heavy." When she finished pushing the ark in place, she sat on its ramp and heaved a big sigh.

After a few moments of silence, Opus asked, "Felicity, are you okay?"

"I'm okay. I just need a minute to catch my breath."

"All right. Take your time."

"Ooof!" A moment later he heard her struggle, and then there was a knock from above. Looking up, he saw her smiling and waving at him. As she looked down for a moment, there was suddenly a *thump, rattle*. One of the controllers landed on top of his head.

"Ow! Hey, I wasn't expecting that."

"Sorry. Watch out, here comes the next one."

"Okay, I'm ready." *Bonk. Thud. Ooof!* With a loud clatter, Opus hit the floor.

"Are you hurt?" Felicity asked as she peeked over the wall. Opus lay on the floor, hopelessly tangled up in his strings. She could not help but laugh at his predicament.

Relieved to be down, although stranded, he looked up at her and glared. "A little help, please." She carefully climbed down and made her way back to the front of the stage.

Standing at the end of the stage with her hand on her hip, she taunted, "I can't leave you alone for a minute," and burst into a new round of giggles.

Indignant, he said, "If you are quite through." He held up a tangle of strings and waved them at her.

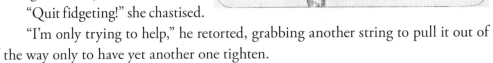

Felicity energetically stepped on to the stage and tottered a little. Spurts of snickers escaped her as she proceeded to untangle him. The tangles seemed endless, and both were getting frustrated. Every time he moved, a different string tightened. It was especially irritating when it happened to strings she had just loosened.

"Quit fidgeting!" she chastised.

"I'm only trying to help," he retorted, grabbing another string to pull it out of the way only to have yet another one tighten.

She smacked his hand and said, "Stop it! Stop it! Don't move! I'll have you out of this in a minute."

He lay there stiffly brooding while she, with only one hand and a stump, painstakingly untied him. "There! All finished." She crossed her arms and surveyed her work.

Opus stood up slowly, testing his new freedom by stretching way up high. "Ahh, thanks. That's so much better. I had a crick in my back." He was elated to be finally free of hanging. He smiled goofily at Felicity. "I would give you a hug, but I don't want us to get tangled up like the last time. So a thank you, milady, will have to do." And he gracefully bowed to her.

"We should still be careful," said Felicity. "Why don't you go first, and I'll make my way around you? I want to get a good look around before it is too dark."

Opus followed Felicity off the stage. He was a little wobbly and giggled at himself for his imbalance. He tested his minor freedom and wrapped his arm around his strings, dragging the controllers off the stage.

They found the easiest way to make a perch to stand on was to roll the toy ark over to the window. So they closed up the ramp and turned it around. It was heavy work but much easier with the two of them working together. First, they pulled their controllers close to the ark to create some slack. Then they pushed the ark toward the window until their strings became taut again. They dragged the controllers to the ark to make slack in their strings, and when the ark was in position under the window, the puppets lowered the ramp. Opus helped Felicity up the ramp. He crawled up after her, and they just sat there for a while and rested.

"I never realized how weak we really were," he said with a rasp of breath. Opus could hear the workmen talking to each other outside. He saw how tired Felicity was. "Just rest while I have a look-see."

He spied down at the workmen from his perch and noted a few pickups, a trailer with a bulldozer on it, and tools scattered around. In the distance he saw the trees and mountains against the pale blue of the twilight sky.

The men below were moving about, and one of the men yelled, "Hey, Mack, where do you want us to start the fires?"

"We'll start 'em at the back and work toward the exit. I want a controlled burn, so the walls will fall in on themselves. We don't want this burn to get out of control," was the answer.

Felicity could hear the men and what they were saying. It made her feel forlorn. She touched Opus with her arm stump for comfort. "Opus, it sounds hopeless."

Keeping a watchful eye out the window, he reached down to her and replied, "We still have each other, and that counts the most."

"But I'm so weak. I don't know if I can go on." She moaned.

He looked at her and saw how frightened she was because she felt her life was near its end. He knelt down and put his hand on her shoulders. "I still have enough hope for the both of us. Have faith in our little friends." As poorly as she felt, she gave him a wan smile. He returned the smile and stroked her cheek. "Remember what Grandpa always said: 'It's always darkest before the dawn.'" And just then, the sky darkened as the sun set below the horizon.

R. S. Rayborn

CHAPTER 6
DARK OMEN

The sun had sunk behind the mountains, and in the twilight, a dark cloud formed where the sun had been. Cold air fell through the broken window, and Felicity shivered.

Opus stared out of the opening at the darkened horizon. The black cloud grew larger and seemed to undulate as it approached. The movement seemed strange since there was no wind to push the dark floating mass toward them. Was this an omen of their doom?

"Felicity?" Opus asked for attention as he pointed into the distance outside. "What is that?"

Just as Felicity arose to look, a bevy of fairies slipped through the broken window. The puppets ducked down onto the ark and watched the flow of fey folk fill the attic.

Opus and Felicity watched Tulip and a bigger fairy fly over them and disappear around the front of the theater box. "Tulip," Opus called out. "We're over here!"

With a worried look, Tulip peeked around the corner of the box. When she spotted her new friends, relief brightened upon her face, and she launched herself at the puppets. Tulip bowled them over and smothered them with hugs and butterfly kisses.

"I missed you sooo much. I was really frightened when I didn't see you in your box. I feared the noisy giants came back and had hurt you or taken you away!" Tulip prattled on, barely taking a breath between her words. "I went with Amelia and spoke to Solomon and Julia, and we have a plan. Amelia's off to get some sawdust from those nasty ol' skyads, and you know how skyads can be."

"Tulip," Julia interrupted. "maybe you should introduce us to your charming new friends."

A now blushing and modest Tulip let go of her friends and stood up with the grace of a young lady in charm school. She clasped her hands in front of her and made introductions. "This is Julia, our eminent seneschal, and matriarch to the passion fairies of the Beaver Dam Valley clan." Then with a smile that matched the morning sunshine, Tulip flitted between Felicity and Opus and held their hands close to her. "These are my new friends, Opus and Felicity."

Not sure what to do in front of high personage, Felicity stepped forward and daintily curtsied.

"How do you do, Felicity?" Julia reached over and helped Felicity stand back up. She held Felicity's hand in hers warmly.

Caught off guard, Felicity sputtered, "I do very well your high … your maj … um!"

"No need for titles. Please, just call me Julia."

"Thank you, Julia." Felicity returned Julia's warmth.

Opus stood there, mouth agape, stunned by Julia's beauty. Tulip had to nudge him forward. "Um, it's a pleasure to meet me, I mean you." After a moment, he regained his composure and performed a perfect bow before her, the consummate actor and gentleman. "I apologize for any faux pas I may have committed." He stepped forward and took her hand in his. "Your beauty blinded me for a moment," he said most charmingly. He bowed again over her hand and kissed it as Felicity rolled her eyes and wondered, *Won't Opus ever learn?*

Julia was all aflutter. She strongly felt the reaction to Opus she would have felt for a human man with a pure heart. Automatically, she turned on her female fairy charms to test his sincerity.

Julia did not let go of Opus's hands as she drew nearer to him and placed her other hand warmly upon his cheek. She stared deeply into his eye, captivating him, and peered deep into his spirit. Julia felt the ebb and surge of his life force, and the energy from the many tender souls who touched and blended into whom Opus the puppet had become.

When Tulip realized what Julia was doing, she turned green with jealousy. She stood seething between them and tried to break Julia's hypnotic gaze by loudly saying, "The noisy giants are going to burn this dwelling down while you are making goo-goo eyes at Opus!"

Unfazed by Tulip's interruption, Julia held Opus's gaze and said, "No goo-goo eyes! I see the attraction, the charm, and the strong spiritual effect of love that Tulip sees in you."

Julia removed her hand from Opus's face yet held onto his hand. She slowly turned and reached over to place her hand on Felicity's cheek. Felicity had also become affected by Julia's gaze. Julia gazed deep into Felicity's eyes for a moment and found what she was looking for. She smiled warmly at Felicity and said, "You are very lucky." Julia released them both from the hypnotic influence. Opus and Felicity blinked off the feeling of sleep.

Julia turned to the assemblage of fey and issued her commands. "Listen, we have a lot to do and a very short time to do it. I want you all in your regular chore groups for these tasks at hand. Agate wing will organize the flight crews. Dahlia crew, find and set up candles and firefly lanterns so we can see to work. Ten join

Beryl wing, for forage and gathering. Beryl wing, when you and Dahlia wing are loaded up, I want you to take the loads out to the lee side of that copse on the side of that field we passed by earlier. Beryl, I want you to organize the drop-off area, and Dahlia's workers will direct the rest of us to the location. The rest of the crews will take their leads from Agate wing."

The gathering shifted around for a moment, trying to absorb all they had heard. Julia bellowed, "Well, get to it!" The fairies shot up into a swirl of wings and myriad swarming bodies.

Julia turned her attention back to Tulip. "Tulip, you mentioned something about a sewing box. Go get what you need to help Opus and Felicity." Tulip snapped to attention and flew off. Julia smiled with excitement at the puppets before she turned back to her following and called out, "I need Prunella here now!"

The call went out, repeated from fairy to fairy till it reached Prunella, who was happily upside down, rummaging through a box. She was doing her best to ignore the swirl of activity outside the box.

"Here she is," yelled a young fairy, pointing at a box. All you could see of Prunella were her two legs waggling about.

Prunella was in heaven as she continued to rummage. Her bliss was interrupted when several pairs of hands grasped her legs and tugged and pulled until finally she popped out of the box. As she emerged, she tightly clutched a prize. She held a magnifying glass as they flew upside down over to Julia and gently plopped the indignant sage down.

"Why is it that every time I have a chance to study noisy giant artifacts you have an emergency?" Prunella asked in a high snit.

Julia turned Prunella around to face the puppets. "Prunella, these are Opus and Felicity."

Prunella adjusted her glasses and studied the puppets with her new prize. "Ah, yes, I see. They are made of wood to move about. Put a pair of wings on them, and they could almost be fairy kind."

Tulip returned, sporting a pink ribbon tied around her waist. A pair of small scissors was stuck in her pink sash on one side, and a huge sewing needle was stuck on the other side.

"Well done, Tulip, praised Julia. "You will be in charge of getting Opus and Felicity ready to travel. Oh, and help Prunella if she needs it."

"Thank you, Julia, for coming to our rescue." Opus sincerely expressed his gratitude.

Julia smiled coquettishly at him. "If you will pardon me, my duties are over there," she explained as she indicated the tumultuous chaos behind her. "I leave you in most capable hands." Reluctantly, she departed.

"Well," Prunella said, "now that little Miss Woo Woo is out of the way, I can get to work. Tulip, get some help, and bring over some of those colorful blocks for my patients to sit on." When the chore was completed, Prunella used the magnifying glass as a pointer. "You two, sit here." The puppets promptly obeyed. As she walked around and peered at them through the magnifying glass, she stumbled over Opus's lap. He automatically put his arms around her to keep her from falling. "Well," she said, looking into Opus's eye, "aren't you the charmer?" Then she smiled at him and blushed.

Tulip snickered behind her hand. Prunella glowered at the little imp.

"Come on, you rogue. Let her up so she can finish her examination." Felicity reached over and pulled one of Opus's arms from around Prunella.

"Wait a moment! While I'm here, I might as well have a look at that eye." Prunella lifted her magnifying glass, and Opus's eye became huge. "Yes, I think I see the problem, but first things first. Tulip," she called as she arose and straightened her dress, "let's get rid of these strings. They're in my way." With that pronouncement, she walked around Opus, grabbed his head string, and pulled it straight up.

Tulip approached Opus and slowly took out her scissors. "Don't move, okay?" she told him nervously.

"Okay," he responded, "I won't budge."

A little aquiver, she asked, "Are you ready?"

"Yes!"

Squinting her eyes closed and turning her head away, Tulip shakily operated the scissors.

"Open your eyes," Prunella yelled. Snip. A startled Tulip cut the string and then dropped the scissors. She covered her face with her hands, frightened that she had just hurt her friend. Tulip slowly peeked through her fingers and saw Opus's head drooped forward. Prunella was still standing behind him, holding the rest of the strings above his head.

"Nooo," Tulip wailed and started to bawl into her arms.

Tulip did not see Opus reach up with his hand and slowly run it through his painted hair. He touched the dangling strings and stopped. He grabbed the string and ran his hand to its end. "Yes," he exclaimed loudly.

Tulip looked up to see his beaming face.

As he pulled the string tight, he said," Cut the rest of it off! Please."

In great relief she asked, "It didn't hurt?"

"Nope, not a bit. See?" He moved his head around freely. "Please, Tulip, free me from my bonds."

With restored confidence, Tulip reached down and retrieved her scissors.

"Tulip!" Prunella said sharply, demanding her attention. "This time, dear, try to keep your eyes open."

"Yes, ma'am." And with her eyes wide open, Tulip cut the head string to the nub.

"See, it didn't hurt." Opus showed her by rubbing the top of his head.

With Prunella's help, Tulip deftly cut off the rest of both puppets' strings. Finally, there was a pile of loose threads at their feet.

Felicity slowly stood and shakily stretched. With a big smile, she lifted a corner of her dress and swished it about. Then she attempted a pirouette but sat back down quickly, feeling a little dizzy. "I'm still kinda weak, and this skirt feels like it weighs a ton."

Tulip tucked her scissors in her sash and picked up the hem of Felicity's skirt. "It does seem very stiff and heavy. Let me ask Julia what she thinks we should do."

"Before you run off, Tulip, come here and help me." Prunella had one knee up against Opus's leg and her hand firmly locked around his head, trying to pry his eye open. "Your eye is being stubborn, young man. I need something with leverage to help me."

She looked around for a moment and then spied the large needle in Tulip's sash. Prunella went to her and pulled out the wickedly huge sewing needle. She held it up, examining it with relish.

"Hey, that's mine," Tulip griped and tried to jump up to get it back.

"Now, now, I need it for healing, little one. Now go run your errand to Julia."

"Um," Opus said nervously, "what do you plan to do with that?"

Prunella looked at him with a mischievous little grin. "Don't you no-never mind, mister!" She looked at her prize and caressed it lovingly. "This won't hurt a bit." Then she launched herself at him. Her tongue was sticking out of the corner

R. S. Rayborn

of her mouth as she attacked the closed eye with vengeance. With one arm wrapped securely around his head and her knee on his lap, she held him down.

Opus could do nothing more than flail his arms about and gag. "Rah, argh, ow, ow."

Felicity giggled at the sight. Then suddenly, there was a loud ping, and she saw a small speck of sand fly from Opus's head. Prunella released him and stood back, looking quite pleased with herself.

Opus blinked his eyes a few times. Then he winked them individually. For the first time in ages, he had a good look around with both eyes open. "Wow, I can see clearer. What do you think, Felicity?"

Felicity inspected his newly opened eye. "It looks much brighter than the other eye. It looks good. How does it feel?"

Opus blinked a couple more times. "It feels great!" And in a happy madcap instant, he jumped up, grabbed Prunella in a bear hug, and twirled her around. "Thank you, thank you. Mmmmuwa!" He gave her a spirited smooch on her cheek. She tittered shyly and went rosy all over. Prunella had been caught totally off guard, not used to receiving that kind of affection. No one had kissed her since she was a fledgling, still in the nest, and she enjoyed it.

After he released her hands, Opus went over to chatter at Felicity. Prunella took a deep breath and released it slowly, regaining some of her composure. She slowly fanned herself with the magnifying glass and savored the pleasure of the new experience. She had concluded a long time ago that since she was so nerdy, the love of science was much safer than getting her feelings hurt by love. Having experienced getting picked last for games and parties, she had followed what seemed a safer path. Maybe she could have real friends instead of clockwork ones. She thought she would start with these two puppets, right here, right now.

Opus turned back to Prunella, still overjoyed from her healing. "My eye has been stuck closed for ages. I thought I would never see out of it again. Thank you from the bottom of my heart!"

Smiling, she said sheepishly, "No problem. You're welcome. All in a day's work." She busied herself wiping off the new tool. "We'll fix all your ills as soon as we get you back to our hamlet. Right now, we need to get you ready to travel." She let her gaze drift toward the broken window and said to no one in particular, "Where is that little scamp Amelia with my elixir?"

CHAPTER 7
LIGHT AS A FEATHER

In the meantime, Tulip came upon Julia reprimanding a plump fairy who had been caught stuffing her face with termites instead of working.

"Julia, I need you," Tulip said.

Thankful for the interruption, Julia turned back to the plump fairy and ordered, "Willow, you are now on termite collecting duty. You will catch and cage termites and carry them to the first staging area. No snacking! Do I make myself clear?"

"Yes, ma'am," responded a disciplined Willow. She rushed back to work.

"Please come back with me so I can show you the problem," Tulip beckoned to Julia. They started back to where the puppets were sitting.

Landing near the puppets, Tulip lifted the hem of Felicity's skirt. "They're free from their strings now but very weak. Felicity's dress is very stiff and heavy. Feel it. The weight and coarse material make it hard for her to move around. What can we do, Mother?"

"Hmmm." Julia fingered Felicity's hem. "Do you have lighter clothing underneath?"

"I don't know. I've never looked," Felicity answered.

"Let me look," Tulip offered as she held up the hem of Felicity's skirt and quickly ducked under. "Here we are! One, two, three skirts and knee-length undies."

"Oh, you mean my bloomers," Felicity corrected.

"Bloomers?" Tulip mumbled, her voice muffled as she emerged from under the skirts.

"A lady's underpants," Felicity explained. "Mother told Rachel that a proper lady always wears bloomers."

"Bloomers!" Tulip slowly sounded out the word with wonder. "They're lacy, and the name kinda sounds like a flower."

"Yes, it does," Felicity agreed and grinned at the thought.

"They're pretty. Can I have some?" Tulip asked.

"Now, Tulip," Julia gently reproved.

"I only have the pair I'm wearing," Felicity explained.

"That's okay, I guess." Tulip sounded disappointed. Then she brightened up with an idea. "Hey, maybe later I can get a good look at them and make a whole bunch of new bloomers for everyone."

"That would be just fine, Tulip. But what can we do about my dress right now?" Felicity asked.

"It will have to come off," Julia said with authority. "It is much too heavy to fly in, and you know what they say about a heavy fairy."

"A fat fairy can't fly any farther than you can toss her," Felicity offered. Both Julia and Tulip gasped at the puppet.

"Very good," Julia said approvingly.

"Now let's see." Tulip slipped behind Felicity, untied the apron's bow knot, and slipped the apron off. She made a cut in the skirt and exposed the very stiff laced skirt underneath and set the outer skirt aside. It was so stiff it stood up by itself. As Tulip turned her attention back to the task at hand, the stiff dress and apron disappeared out the window. Slowly, she cut the tie for the skirt, and the springy pleats made it bounce when it fell to the floor. Felicity kicked it out of the way. And it, too, disappeared out the window with the next passing fairy. One more. Tulip cut the waist tie of the slip and helped Felicity step out of it. Felicity was left wearing a long blouse and her bloomers, which were long, billowy, and lacy. The bottoms of the bloomers tied off just above the knee with a nice ruffle. "There! How do you feel now?" Tulip asked.

Felicity lifted her arms and turned about. "I feel better. Free. Almost as if I could float."

Opus studied her new look, smirked, and gave her a little wink. "You look good in bloomers."

Felicity fanned herself with her hand coyly, and with her best Southern belle drawl said, "Well, I do declare, Mr. Opus, you are shameless."

"Okay, Opus. Now it's your turn," Tulip announced.

As she approached him with her scissors, Opus put up his hands to her. "Umm, wait a minute. I don't think I have any underwear on." Opus may have seemed a little modest about his appearance, but he couldn't help it. That's the way he was carved and dressed.

Julia stepped up and said, "We need to lighten you up a bit as we did with Felicity. You're big and strong, so start with the jacket, and we will see how you move about."

Prunella grabbed his arms from behind. She was quite strong for a skinny little thing. "Relax, ya big baby. I promise this won't hurt a bit!"

Tulip removed the belt from the jacket and snipped off the buttons, while Opus protested desperately.

"But, but, but that's what you said the last time—" He didn't get to finish as Prunella reached around him and grabbed his lapel. Like an old bandage, she quickly whisked his coat off, whirling him into a spin. His eyeballs continued to twirl around in their sockets with a whir. Prunella dropped the coat, grabbed Opus's shoulder, and none too gently biffed him on the back of the head. With a click, his eyes instantly stopped spinning and his vision began to focus.

Still a little dizzy and struggling to see normally, he babbled, "Nothing to see here. Move along." He bonked himself on the side of the head with the palm of his hand. "Mommy, may I have another cookie?" Opus shook his head vigorously. "Whubba, whubba, whubba," he said and glared indignantly at Prunella. "I thought you said that wouldn't hurt!"

Smiling, Prunella explained, "I said it won't hurt a bit, and it didn't, did it? It hurt a lot. I am sorry it hurt, but we don't have time to waste." She tittered behind her hand. "Now, let's see how you are doing."

Prunella helped Opus to stand. Gaining his balance, he took a few steps and stretched his arms. His shirttail immediately came untucked, and when he flexed his arms, his sleeves were so tight one ripped at the shoulder. "Oops," said Opus.

"That's okay, Opus. Sit back down so I can fix it." Opus sat down while she carefully snipped the threads at his shoulder. Then she unbuttoned the cuff and slipped the sleeve off. She went to the other shoulder and made quick work of it as well.

When Tulip was done, Opus stood back up and flexed and stretched freely. "Wow, I feel so free!" He started to do a little jig and a spin. "Ooh, I had better be careful not to get dizzy again." He moved over to Felicity, bowed, offered his hand, and smiled. "Would you care to dance, milady?" he asked.

"Why thank you, kind sir." Felicity accepted his hand and was led to a clear space on the floor. Taking their positions, they began to waltz. A flute played in tempo with their steps. Work came to a halt as others fairies joined in with a variety of

pocket instruments. Some clapped, some hummed, and all swayed with the rhythm. The entire assembly of fairies was enjoying the wondrous phenomenon of the puppets displaying their newfound freedom.

At that point, Felicity lost all her strength and collapsed on the floor. The music stopped and was replaced by concerned gasps throughout the attic. Winded, Opus knelt down next to Felicity and Tulip flew to her friend. Julia quickly buzzed over. Tulip sat down and cradled Felicity's head in her lap. Felicity reached up for Opus, and with tears in her eyes, she moaned with weariness. "I'm too tired, Opus. I don't think I can make it."

Opus was breathing hard himself but still had the strength to encourage Felicity. "I'm tired too. But we have to keep trying. Look at all the friends we have helping us." His gaze followed the wave of his hand toward all the fairies. They halted their work and had concerned expressions upon their faces.

Tulip gave Felicity a big hug and said, "We love you, Felicity. You're part of our family now. I won't let anything happen to you!"

CHAPTER 8
SMOKE AND FIRE

Suddenly shrieks echoed from the back of the attic as tendrils of smoke wafted up the stairwell. The entire flock of fairies went into panic and started to swarm toward the window.

Julia raised her voice again and commanded, "Be calm! We have time before the fire reaches here." And they were. Tulip helped Opus and Felicity back to the blocks, so they could sit and rest. More smoke billowed up the attic stairwell, and became denser all over the room.

Opus beckoned to Julia. "I have an idea. There is a door at the bottom of the stairwell. Maybe it can be closed and sealed off to give us more time."

Julia didn't hesitate. She called the fairies to follow her as she went toward the stairs. The cloudy, gray plumes were creating a dense, tear-making fog. A few brave fairies flew into the smoke and down the stairs. You could hear them hack and cough as they struggled to get lower. There was a cheer of relief when they heard the door slam shut. The brave fairies slowly returned out of the murk, squinting through smoke-caused tears. Wet rivulets ran down their ashen faces as their friends quickly helped them to the window for much-needed fresh air.

As the smoke lessened, other fairies replaced the first group down the stairwell. They stuffed rags and fluff in all the cracks and crevices. Most of the fairies in the attic were now coughing because of the smoke.

Julia was covered with soot and choking from her work in the stairwell. "Break that window over there," she ordered, pointing to the unbroken window on the other side of the attic. It took several fairies tree-hard strikes with a brass candlestick to break the window. But with their perseverance and pluck, they finally forced the candlestick through the glass! The sound of the breaking window was heard above the general hubbub, and everyone cheered. The cross-draft quickly provided fresh air and thinned the smoke to a safe level.

One of Julia's protector fairies flew over to confirm. "Mother, the window has been broken, and the smoke will be cleared out soon. There is another problem. Mother, many are complaining that the floor is getting too hot to stand on, and everyone is tired from moving so much stuff. Lastly, I believe it's time for you to fly to safety. It's dangerous in here, and Dixie has threatened to pin my wings back if anything happens to you."

"She did, did she? No, I must stay. There is still much to do."

"But Mother, you mustn't! I can wait for Dixie and—"

"You will organize everyone to grab one last load and lead them to the copse nearby," Julia interrupted. "I want you to tend to the wounded. Get everyone fed and rested. After that, start shifts—one taking loads back, one cleaning, and one resting."

"But, but, Mother!" the protector fairy pleaded.

"No buts! You have your orders. Now fly to it!" The protector fairy saluted and then flew off to begin organizing the troops.

Slowly, the exodus from the attic spiraled into the field. Julia checked the almost empty room to make sure no one was left behind. She spied Tulip standing next to Felicity, rocking from one hot foot to the other, and ordered, "You must leave as well, Tulip!"

"No," Tulip said firmly.

"Tulip!" Julia snapped, mother-like.

"I'm not leaving my friends again," Tulip announced stubbornly.

"Even with a direct order from your matron and seneschal? Julia stated her order with a question.

Tulip gazed down sheepishly at her feet, pondered for a moment, and then nodded. She stepped between the puppets, took hold of their hands, and stated, "I love them too much to abandon them!"

Julia demeanor changed from being very stern to nodding with approval. "I respect that kind of devotion, youngling. You may stay."

"No, you all must go now," Opus insisted. "We have lived a long time and are way past our prime. We love you too much to see you stay and get hurt because of us. Please go."

"And that," Julia replied, "is why we will stay. Because of love."

Julia turned to Tulip. "Go to the sewing box, and bring back some strong thread or heavy twine. We can lower our friends out the window."

After Tulip flew away, Prunella suggested more help was needed to handle the weight. Julia nodded, realizing her oversight. "It will be all right, young one," Prunella teased. "It's just one more life lesson for you."

Tulip flew to the sewing box and peered inside to find it was empty. She despaired for only a moment, and then frantically flew around the attic in search of string. On the far side of the attic, she spotted a rough-looking piece of string that led to underneath a pile of newspapers. She pushed the papers out of the way and found an enormous spool of twine. She tried to pick it up and quickly figured out why it had been left behind. It was way too heavy and ungainly to move. On her second try, Tulip wrapped both her arms around the spool and heaved it up. She fluttered her wings faster, yet it seemed the harder she flapped, the more rooted to the floor she was. Her feet were stinging from the heat, and her wings were tired, so she decided the only option left was to carry it back, walking.

Stooped over with the heavy load, Tulip waddled in the direction of her friends. "Yowtch," she yelped with every step she took. Her feet tingled with pain from the baking floor, like the hot sand at the pond. "Ow, ow," she yelled. Wisps of smoke and flickering light leaked through the gaps in the floorboards. Halfway back, there was a loud creak. She stopped and looked around. Then there was a pop, a snap, and a yell of "Eeek!" as Tulip and the spool fell through a burning hole that had suddenly appeared in the floor.

R. S. Rayborn

CHAPTER 9
SINGED

The fire had weakened the wooden floor so much that the weight of Tulip and the twine had broken through. Smoke and sparks billowed up out of the glowing hole as Tulip screeched, "Yeeowwttch!" She had saved herself by dropping the heavy spool and dodging the roaring flames in the room below.

Flying backwards from the hole as the flames leaped, she looked back as one long tendril of flame reached out for her. "Yikes," she yelled. Singed and frightened, she turned and zoomed back to her friends, leaving a smoking trail.

Julia clutched the little fairy and inspected her for injuries. "Are you all right?"

"No," Tulip whimpered. "I lost the thread and scorched my wings. Look! They're still smoking."

"That's smoke from your wings. It's smoke from your dress! You're still on fire, Tulip." Prunella doused Tulip's backside with water to extinguish the flames. Steam rose up from the dampened fabric.

"Ow! I think I burned my fanny," she whined.

Julia inspected the burn. "Well, you certainly burned a large hole in the backside of your dress."

Prunella treated Tulip's burns and tied her shawl around her patient's waist as a bandage. With her reddened cheeks and bottom anointed and covered, Tulip repeated her earlier complaint. "I lost the twine when I fell through the floor. It was much too heavy for me to fly with, so I let it go."

"A good thing you did, or we would have lost you. And that would have broken my heart," Julia said. Felicity nodded in agreement.

"Now what are we going to do?" Tulip whined and started to sniffle.

"The worst that happened, besides your singed backside, is that your pride has been hurt. On the other hand, we are thankful you are still alive." Prunella said this endearingly and completely out of character for her. Prunella hugged Tulip and kissed the top of her head.

Felicity reached over and squeezed Tulip's hand. "You did valiantly, and I love you for trying. You must all go now. The fire is too big, and it would sadden us if you hurt yourselves anymore on our account. Please go!"

Tulip, in tears, clamped her little arms around Felicity and held on fiercely. "No," she wailed and buried her head into Felicity's shoulder.

Julia realized that the puppets were right; the fire had gained strength. There was nothing else they could do for the puppets here. "I'm sorry, my friends." The smoke made her cough. "But we must go away." After hugging Felicity, Julia pried a crying Tulip away and ordering, "Come along, Prunella." Prunella hesitated. "Prunella!"

Prunella turned away from the puppets with tears staining her cheeks.

With her arms wrapped around the fairy's waist, Julia took off, followed closely by Prunella.

CHAPTER 10
In the Nick of Time!

The three fairies were almost to the smoke-filled window when Dixie and Amelia burst in at top speed.

Tulip broke free of Julia's grasp and flew straight to Amelia. With a tear-stained face, she chided her friend. "Where have you been, young lady?" Tulip stood there, hands on hips, glaring at her best friend. Then she broke down and flung her arms around Amelia. She hugged her so tightly, she lifted her right off the floor.

Amelia returned her friend's hug and was a little shocked at Tulip's disheveled appearance. "And what adventures have you been having?" Amelia asked. "Has there been a lot of excitement without me, and now I can't call you scaredy frog anymore?"

Tulip pouted at Amelia and pointed to her rear. "I burned my little fanny!"

Amelia giggled and then inspected and worried over Tulip's singed wings. "Oh, Tulip, your wings are scorched. Let me see what I can do about that."

Tulip stopped Amelia from fussing over her. "Right now we need to help Opus and Felicity. Did you bring it?"

Amelia proffered a large buttercup bag with liquid sloshing around in it. Tulip grabbed the bag, walked over to Felicity, and told her to drink. Felicity swallowed deeply, feeling the elixir saturate her dry, wooden insides. Slowly, she began to feel it invigorate her.

Amelia squeezed Felicity, which made her dribble drops of the precious elixir on her blouse. Then she went over to give Opus a hug.

Meanwhile, Dixie was reporting to

Julia. "We dropped off the sawdust to be mixed up and then flew straight here as fast as our wings could carry us."

"You arrived just in time, but we have another problem. All the spools of thread were taken out, and Tulip almost lost her life trying to carry the last spool over here," Julia explained.

"I was wounded. See." Tulip turned her poor burned bottom toward Dixie, pointing. "Hey, will I get a Pansy Heart Medal for being wounded in battle?"

Julia frowned at Tulip and tousled her hair. She caught Dixie's attention and pointed at the flaming hole in the middle of the attic floor. As they stared at the glowing conflagration, a trunk tipped into the hole and caused a shower of sparks to burst up to the rafters. The smoke and heat in the attic were becoming unbearable.

"Wait!" Felicity's eyes shined with a wild idea that just popped into her head. "Where are our controller strings?"

Prunella quickly picked up the idea and agreed excitedly. "Right here on the floor! Tulip, Amelia, Dixie come help me! Tulip, cut those strings from the controllers. When she's done, start tying them together."

The fairies snapped to work. Tulip cut the strings, and the rest of them proceeded to untangle the mess. When enough strings were free, Dixie and Amelia tied them together.

Prunella told Tulip, "You will need something with a little weight to tie to the end that goes out the window. It will pull the line all the way to the ground and keep the line taut down below. We will also need something really heavy to secure the other end of the line in here. We don't want to lose the line when we throw out the little weight."

"I think I've found something for the little weight," Amelia called out.

Tulip flew over and gasped, "Are those teeth?"

"Yes! Noisy giant teeth!" Amelia replied.

"Wow, they're so big! I didn't know noisy giants could take their teeth out," Tulip said with surprise.

They had found Grampa's old lower set of false teeth. Amelia tied the end of the string tightly with square knots.

Tulip had chosen the ark for the anchor weight, and tied her end of the string through the windows of the toy boat. "Okay, I'm done. How are Opus and Felicity doing?"

Opus was drinking deeply from the elixir bag, when Tulip and Amelia brought the false teeth over with the line trailing behind. Felicity sat up straighter and looked more energetic than ever.

"How do you feel?" Tulip asked.

"Stronger," Felicity replied.

"Great! All we have to do now is throw this out the window, and you can escape."

"Good," Julia said, "because it's way past time for us all to leave!"

Opus stopped drinking and let out a loud burp. He handed the buttercup bag back to Julia. "Thank you. That really hits the spot."

"Tulip, here, take a drink." Julia pushed the bag into Tulip's hands, and she gulped down the tonic thirstily. When she stopped, she gasped a couple of times and then made a dainty little girl burp. "Excuse me," she said coyly and giggled behind her hands.

"Amelia," Julia called out. "Come here."

"I'm almost finished," she said, coughing. "I'll be right there." Amelia appeared out of the haze, teary-eyed.

"Here, drink this." As Julia helped her with the bag, Amelia swallowed and sputtered a little before she stopped drinking. The cool liquid cleared her throat, and her head cleared. She felt stronger, more alive, and ready for more challenges.

"Wow! That's some drink," she exclaimed.

"It has queen bee honey and certain herbs," Julia explained. Julia then turned to Dixie and Prunella, who were arranging the last of the strings. "Your turn, Dixie."

Dickie was lugging the noisy giant's partial dentures to the window. Without looking back, she said, "I'm kinda busy. Just get those two ready to move," she said testily.

"Amelia, take this elixir to Dixie, and tell her to drink it. Or I'll have Cookie dose her with extra castor oil when we get back home. I'm sure she recalls how Cookie is when it comes to castor oil."

Amelia obeyed and quickly flew the bag over to Dixie with Julia's message.

Dixie shot Julia a nasty glare, took the buttercup bag, and drank. Prunella came over to make sure Dixie complied with Julia's order. She smiled smugly when Dixie finished and tossed the bag to Prunella, saying, "Your turn!"

Prunella left the brooding protector fairy to finish her task, grinned broadly, and drank the elixir.

Felicity was wobbling to her feet with some help from Tulip. Opus stood up on his own, and he and the fairy both helped Felicity get to the window.

After Dixie finished her task, she flew over and grabbed the elixir bag from Prunella with a mischievous grin. She thrust the bag at Julia. "Mothers are not exempt from Cookie's castor oil. It's your turn now," Dixie commanded.

Julia smiled at Dixie and rolled her eyes at Prunella, who just crossed her arms and waited. Julia drank the elixir and instantly felt better for doing it.

"Are you strong enough?" Dixie asked as she appraised Opus's posture and movements.

"I'd better be," he responded. "Felicity, how do you feel?"

"I'm getting stronger by the minute," she replied. "Let's get out of here!"

"Here!" Julia put the elixir bag in Felicity's hands. "Drink more, both of you! Finish it if you can. It will increase your endurance for the trip home." The puppets took turns finishing off the contents of the bag. They could feel their life force quickening and increasing dramatically.

Wiping his mouth with his arm, Opus said, "I'm going down first. When I reach the ground, send Felicity down." Then he told Dixie, "You may need to help me over the edge."

Dixie shoved Opus up and over. He snagged the left knee of his trousers on a jagged piece of glass and ripped a large hole there. He steadied himself and clutched the string tightly to control his descent. Looking at Felicity, he warned, "Be careful when you come out. Wrap the string around your elbow and under your rear to slow yourself as you slide. See you soon!" Opus disappeared into the darkness below.

On the way down, Opus glanced in the second-story window at the roaring flames. The devastation was frightening. Flames and smoke licked at him through the cracks as he passed by. When he finally hit the ground, he was exhilarated. He gave the string a couple of tugs and yelled, "I'm down! Send Felicity quickly. The fire is growing."

Felicity wound the string around her arm once and carefully climbed out the window. Placing the string under her rump, she held the other end in her good hand. Taking a couple of baby steps backward, she loosened a little string at a time and slowly descended.

With Felicity safely on her way down and flames licking at their wings, the fairies left the window like comets, streaking through the opening and into the fresh air.

When Felicity reached the second-story window, she, too, stopped and stared at the inferno within. Fascinated, she watched as the flames totally consumed the children's bedroom. The hole that Tulip had fallen through had widened so much she could see into the attic. Shaking with fear, she realized how close their end had been. She watched as the little theater box tumbled into the blaze and looked away quickly. The air was so hot the tears she cried instantly dried upon her cheek. Suddenly, the ark slipped and played out too much line.

Opus was startled when the string he held suddenly went slack. He stepped away from the wall and looked up in time to see Felicity slide down and jerk when the line went taut. Then the line snapped, and she came tumbling down. As he fearfully gauged her descent,

Opus reached out with anxious determination and caught Felicity in his arms. Well, almost. When Opus caught her, the force of her weight knocked him to the ground, and he landed hard on his wooden bottom. Despite the crash, he never let Felicity go, and he hugged her fiercely to his chest.

"Oh, darling, I thought for a moment I had lost you!" He felt her shoulders and gave her a quick once-over for injuries and hugged her again with relief. "Nothing broken? I was so worried. I don't know what I would have done if you had died before I could tell you I love you! Felicity? Speak to me honey I—"

Felicity interrupted him with a long passionate kiss. Even though he was shocked at first, he kissed her back with equal fervor.

Felicity always knew she loved Opus, even from the moment she had awakened that first Christmas. But she didn't know if he loved her back. Oh, they had always been the best of friends, and that is how he had treated her, as a friend. Now, with his declaration, she knew he loved her, and she still loved him. So she said so. "I love you, Opus." For a moment, they said nothing and gazed lovingly into each other's eyes.

CHAPTER 11
ON THE RUN

"Ow!" Opus turned Felicity over and covered her with his body as flying glass showered the area. A window above the puppets had blown out. Flames roared out the window, illuminating the night sky.

"What was that?" came a shout from the other side of the house.

The fairies swooped down and helped the puppets up. The little group rushed for the nearest cover, a parked pickup. They had just made it under the truck and tucked themselves into shadows when three noisy giants appeared from around the corner of the burning house. The three workmen inspected the area to make sure everything was all right.

One of the noisy giants walked over to the pickup and walked around it. "I don't see any damage. Just a bit of glass on the hood." He kicked the tire he was standing next to. "Tire's fine." The roar of the flames muffled a couple of quiet squeaks from behind the tire.

Prunella placed her hand over Tulip's mouth to stifle her sounds of fear as the three men left.

Felicity sat in front of Opus, his arms wrapped around her protectively. The puppets watched as their home for many years was engulfed in flames.

"Opus, our home," Felicity shuddered and moaned sadly. She leaned her head back onto Opus's shoulder, and her tears ran freely.

Tulip freed herself from Prunella so she could help comfort Felicity. "Felicity, home isn't just a place you hang your hat. Or in your case, hang in a box." Tulip gave Felicity a hug and smiled up at her. "Home is where you're loved." She squeezed Felicity, pressing her cheek into Felicity's blouse. Amelia felt moved and joined in the hug. Then Julia and even Prunella added their hugs.

At last, Dixie came over and included them all with her hug, and she started to sniffle. Prunella and Julia gazed in surprise at Dixie's emotional outbreak and smiled at her straightening herself. Dixie admitted, "Well, all this hugging and lovey-dovey stuff is contagious. Almost like catching a cold." Then she moved off into the shadows.

The hugging group laughed. Felicity wiped the tears from her smiling cheeks.

An anxious Dixie, with spear in hand, reappeared out of the darkness. She squeezed Opus's arm, and in a low urgent tone said, "We need to leave."

Julia took command. "Dixie, you and Amelia fly scout. Tulip and I will stay on the ground with Opus and Felicity. Prunella, head straight to our hamlet, and tell Solomon what has happened. And prepare for our arrival." The three fairies acknowledged their assignments and disappeared into the night.

Tulip contradicted Julia's command and said in her most authoritative voice, "Follow me!" Then she exaggerated her sneakiness as she slinked away.

"Well, follow her," Julia said with a wry grin and motioned the puppets to follow the leader. Julia took the rear guard and whispered loudly to Tulip, "Be careful, and watch your step."

Then the small object Julia stepped on moved, and she fell. "Yipe," Julia yelled. Something shaggy yipped and shot up from the darkness. Julia had stepped on the end of a hairy tail. The tail was attached to a large, shaggy, and very startled dog, who jumped excitedly. When the dog landed, it looked confused and scared as he snapped his jaws at the surrounding darkness. The hound was a big, vicious-looking brute, with a wide spiked collar and a long leash that trailed behind him. Not a foot away from the angry cur, Julia was sprawled out on the ground, frozen with fear. With its hackles up, the dog emitted a deep, low, rumbling growl and peered menacingly at Julia.

Opus yelled out, "Hey!" He threw a small stone that hit the dog on the neck. The dog snapped at the new threat and turned its face toward Opus. The distraction gave Julia the moment she needed to leap into the air and away from the threat. The dog lunged and snapped at the moving target. He kept trying to catch Julia in his jaws, but she was too fast for him and kept out of reach.

While the dog's attention was on Julia. Opus yelled for the others to run. Tulip took flight and dragged poor Felicity along as well as she could. Felicity ran with her feet barely touching the ground. Trailing behind, Opus picked up a stick almost as tall as he and readied himself for trouble. Julia had tried to keep the barking dog turning in circles, taunting him, but he caught sight of the fleeing trio. Realizing the prey in front of him was not so easy, he turned toward the fleeing puppets.

The trio had a good head start into the thicket. They kept running as the beast gained on them and snapped at their heels. Opus swung his stick with gusto at the chomping jaws. With a surge of speed, the dog was able to clamp his teeth into the seat of Opus's pants, and violently flung him to the side of the trail.

Felicity screamed. She pulled herself free of Tulip and rushed back to help Opus. The dog was running so fast he missed Felicity and slid out of control for several feet. By the time he recovered, Felicity had picked up Opus's stick and hovered protectively over him. As the beast snapped and growled at her, she swung the club back and forth, holding the dog at bay. The dog slowly circled around them, looking for the chance to pounce.

Just as the dog lunged, Dixie zoomed in and with a mighty throw, released her spear. The spear missed the dog and hit its target. The spear went through the leash's loop and buried itself deep in the ground. The dog was brought up short inches from his prey as the leash went taut. Shaking off the sudden stop, the dog strained at the leash, snarling and slobbering with frustration.

Tulip zoomed in and looked sternly into the snarling dog's eyes. She hovered a mere inch from those snapping jaws. She smacked the dog hard on the nose, making it yelp. "That will be quite enough out of you!" she commanded. Shocked, surprised, and hurt, the dog cowed and whimpered under Tulip's fobbing gaze. "Now you just stay there and be good," she ordered. The dog whimpered.

"I feel awful," Opus complained.

"You were just attacked by that vicious brute," Felicity responded. "I can't imagine you would feel like dancing an Irish jig."

"Are you hurt, Opus?" Tulip asked as she fluttered over.

"I'll live," Opus replied, "but my shirt and pants are ripped to shreds," he said, looking at his clothing.

Dixie flew over and landed. She eyed the dog warily and asked, "You want me to dispatch the cur?"

"Oh, no," said Tulip. She flew over and landed in front of the dog, who was still cowering. She faced Dixie with a defiant, protective stance. "You are not going to hurt him. Look at him. He's just a big puppy."

The dog looked sad and penitent. Tulip took pity on the doggy and spoked baby talk to him. "Aw, you just haven't been loved right. have you? Here." And to the astonishment of the others, Tulip walked to the cowering dog's head and scratched him behind his ear. A big contented smile formed on the dog's muzzle. Then his back leg started to thump the ground. "That means he's happy, like wagging his tail," Tulip said as she continued to soothe the doggy with pets, hugs, and the removal of a flea from the dog's ear. It gave everyone else time to recover from their recent scare.

Julia marveled at Tulip's skill in dealing with the mangy, flea-ridden mongrel.

Tulip dutifully combed her fingers through the dog's coat, picking fleas out and popping them between her fingers. "Nasty ol' fleas have probably been making you miserable for years." The dog barked and then licked her face in one big slurp.

"Whew, I feel worse than I did before," Opus said tiredly as he slowly stood up and wobbled.

"Not many have survived an attack like that," Julia commiserated.

"Maybe, but that is not what I mean. I feel worn out! Worn down, and out of energy. I don't know how far I'll be able to go," he explained.

"I know what you mean, Opus. I feel it too," Felicity agreed. "It's as if whatever the fairies gave us to drink ran out of energy."

Tulip was now getting appreciative doggy licks. "Okay, Dixie, you can release him now," Tulip said.

"Are you sure?" Dixie asked.

"Sure I'm sure. Watch this." Tulip took Opus's stick from Felicity and waved it back and forth in front of the doggy. "Wanna play fetch, boy?" The dog jumped up like a puppy, wagging its tail, hopping up and down and back and forth.

Dixie was still not sure. So when she pulled her spear free, she took a battle-ready stance.

Tulip teased and taunted the doggy to play. "Okay, boy, ya want it? Huh? Ya want it, boy?" The dog woofed. "Yes, you do. Yes, you do. Come on. Come on. Go get it!" She tossed the stick far back toward the house. The dog leaped toward it in hot pursuit. "Well," Tulip said, wiping her hands together to clean them, that takes care of that."

A large gob of drool landed on Tulip's shoulder. She realized that the dog had reappeared and was standing directly over her. The stick was clenched in his smiling muzzle, and his tail was wagging madly. He dropped the slobbery stick on Tulip's head and then crouched down, expectantly awaiting his next turn."

Julia said in exasperation, "Now you've done it! He's adopted you." With a frantic wave of her hand, she decreed, "He's your responsibility now. You feed him and clean up after him. And control his fleas."

"If we're done with the attack now, can we get going? Opus asked weakly. He looked as if in pain as he took a couple of steps forward and stumbled.

"Are you hurt? You can't walk like that," Felicity said as she helped Opus steady himself.

"No, no. I think I'm okay. I'm just really tired," he explained.

"So am I," said Felicity. "All the excitement has totally drained us." She agreed with Opus, feeling very listless herself.

With a deep sigh, Julia said, "There aren't enough of us to carry even one of you. And we're tired too."

The dog barked at Tulip, begging her to throw the stick again. He was making a ruckus, eager to play again. "Hush him up, Tulip. I need to think," Julia commanded. The dog kept barking as Julia paced back and forth, rubbing her temples, trying to push away the headache that she felt coming on.

"Tulip, he's getting on my nerves!" Julia shut her eyes and covered her ears.

"Wait a minute, Mother," Tulip said, tugging on Julia's arm. "I have an idea." Tulip walked over to the dog and commanded him to sit. "Now behave yourself." Tulip turned back and addressed the little group. "How about the dog? He is big and strong enough to carry Opus and Felicity, and he's full of energy."

"Yes! That is a brilliant idea, Tulip." Julia was excited now. "Come on, let's help them climb on the dog."

Tulip kept the dog still and talked to him about what they were going to do. "Now be good. My friends need help, so we're going to ride you all the way to my home. I'll hang on your ears and guide you. Would you like that, boy? Huh? You wanna come live with me?" The dog crouched down on his front paws and wagged his tail in the air wildly. Tulip hugged his head and kept on talking to him.

As the puppets climbed on the dog's back, Dixie wrapped the leash around his chest and tied it. "This is for you to hang on to," she explained to Opus.

Felicity sat behind Opus and wrapped her arms around him. He grabbed the leash and tucked his feet into the dog's collar for stability.

Julia gave Tulip some last-minute instructions. "Tulip, guide the dog, and make sure he doesn't go too fast. We don't want anybody falling off."

Tulip flitted up to the dog's head and took a seat right behind his ears. She whispered into his ear, and he gave an acknowledging woof. "Okay, Mother. We're ready to go."

Julia nodded once and took to the air.

CHAPTER 12
It Would Be Easier if You Could Fly

The dog bounded up the trail as Opus and Felicity hung on for dear life. The passage up the mountain was long and arduous, yet surprisingly uneventful. It would have been much easier if the puppets and the dog had wings, and they could have saved themselves the bumpy ride by flying. When the group finally crested the mountaintop, the dog plopped down in exhaustion. Rolling clouds lazily moved across the sky and revealed a full moon past the zenith.

"Look." Tulip pointed down into the misty vale. The luminous glow reflected on a sparking stream that glistened like jewels through the wisps of haze.

The valley was covered in shadows and nighttime mist. Dots of small fires could be seen near a glimmering pond.

Julia appeared out of nowhere, positively aglow. She announced to the puppets, "Welcome to the hamlet of Beaver Dam Valley."

The wonderful smell of cooked food wafted through the air moved by Julia's wings. Tulip's stomach rumbled, and the dog's stomach rumbled in agreement.

Julia flew to Tulip, gave her a hug, and patted the hungry dog's tummy. "We'll be there soon," Julia said. "Then you can eat and go directly to the nest for a well-earned rest. Now, see if you can encourage your ride down the last leg of our journey."

Tulip hugged the dog's neck. "Just a little way further, boy. Then we can eat and sleep. Come on, boy. Up we go."

It took them a good hour to reach the cook fires. The fires had been made near the base of a huge tree. Opus and Felicity climbed down and walked stiffly to Prunella, who was stifling a yawn and trying to stir several large iron pots at the same time.

Her helpers—in fact, all fey folk—had passed out from exhaustion. They were lying about all over the area, having made as comfortable a bed as they could. They used cloth and clothing from the attic and leaves and grass to make soft spots. Some were curled around the limbs of trees and in the nooks of rocks. Even lily pads made waterbeds for some.

Above the sounds of sleepers and girly snores, something big was snoring up in the dark boughs of the tree. It was so big that whenever it took a breath, you could hear it make the tree creak and groan.

"Here." Prunella brought their attention back to the present by ladling out food into bowls and passing them around. She even provided one for the dog.

The dog wolfed down his food and licked his lips appreciatively as his tail swung happily. The simple stew was perfectly delicious and very filling to the exhausted troop.

"There is a nest made up for you over there," Prunella said as she waved her hand toward the base of the huge tree. Opus led Felicity over to the tree and they saw, in between the crook of two root legs, a large nest made of moss and old cloth.

With full bellies, everyone felt very sleepy. Opus and Felicity, Amelia, and Tulip shuffled into the nest, and after snuggling into the soft moss, fell fast asleep. The dog curled up at the foot of the nest and repeated parts of the journey with dreams of running!

Chapter 13
Home at Last

Felicity awakened late the next morning to the permanently smiling face of Berry Bear, nose to nose with her. She felt something moving on her leg and sat up. There was Tulip, stretching a cloth measuring tape along her body. "What in the world are you doing, Tulip?"

"Measuring you," Tulip answered matter-of-factly. She still had ashes and stains on her face and clothing. Prunella's dirty shawl was still wrapped around her waist, and burn marks showed all over her wings and clothing.

Tulip flashed Felicity a winning smile. "Good morning, sleepyhead," she said as she hopped out of the nest and ran off. Felicity sat there and watched her go with the measuring tape fluttering after.

The talking and movement woke Opus. The first thing he saw wasn't a beautiful smile but a bear's rump in his face. He shied away from it as his eyes focused and he realized what it was. He batted Berry Bear to the foot of the nest, where the bear came to rest, sitting up and smiling mischievously. Opus yawned and stretched, and looked all around the haven.

"Good morning, Felicity," Opus said. "Boy, I sure slept well, but I feel as stiff as a board. Do you have any idea what time of day it is?"

"It looks like we sleep in," she said, tilting her head to him. "It's a beautiful day to wake up and be in love." And it was. The sun was out. The birds were singing, and so were all of the fey folk. With nary a cloud in the sky, the sun streamed warmly through the branches of the huge tree.

All around, fey folk were sorting and cleaning the things brought back from the attic. Many were splashing, washing, and playing in the pond. With all the happy activity, Felicity felt at peace. The memory of the attic and the fire seemed like a dream a million years ago. It hardly seemed possible that only yesterday they were stuck in their little theater box in that dark attic.

Felicity watched Prunella, who looked haggard from lack of sleep. Much to the annoyance of the other sages and cooks, she was still supervising the simmering cauldrons. They argued with Prunella, trying to convince the exhausted fairy to go to bed and stop being a pain in the wings. The mix of voices and clatter was like the noise of a gaggle of geese and filled Felicity with glee.

The relative quiet was broken when a deep baritone voice spoke to the puppets from above. "Well, good morning, little cousins." With pops and creaks, Solomon bent his huge trunk to peer down upon the little puppets. "How do you do. My name is Solomon."

Felicity fainted! Several moments later, she came to and felt soothing hands holding her and a cool washcloth on her forehead. Opus cradled her close as she anxiously grasped his forearm and whispered. "Did you see that?"

"Yes, yes. It's okay," he said, totally unruffled. "We were just introduced to Solomon, the grandfather of all trees."

"Did that shaggy old acorn scare you?" Amelia joined in to help calm Felicity's shattered nerves. "Why, he's as gentle and cuddly as Tulip's Berry Bear."

"Come on. Up we go." Opus helped Felicity to stand. "Let us help you. Come over here, so you can get a better look." Opus and Amelia guided Felicity a few paces away from the base of the tree. They turned, and Opus pointed up the trunk. Felicity saw a huge, kind, elderly face smiling down on them.

"I'm sorry, little cousin. I did not mean to frighten you," Solomon apologized.

Opus made the introduction. "Solomon, this is my fiancée, Felicity."

Felicity swayed in dumbfounded silence. She was not really sure what to think or do next. Keeping her eyes on the face of the king of trees, she gave a small and awkward curtsy.

"No need for that, little cousin. We are all family here. I can see the signs of your escape. Look at you! You're soot-covered and singed, and you all look like you survived a forest fire," Solomon observed.

"Well, we did escape our burning house," Felicity explained. "It was just horrible to watch the little we had and our home consumed in flames." Felicity trembled with the emotion of the memory.

Tulip reappeared with her measuring tape. With some difficulty, she hovered in front of Felicity. "Hold still," she said as she measured Felicity's head. Finishing, she landed with a thud and wiped sweat from her forehead.

Solomon groaned in surprise. "Tulip, you're injured!"

Tulip stood there and hung her head low, feeling ashamed. She was not sure why she was in trouble, but it was always safe to act abashed, until you knew why you were in trouble. At least that's what Amelia always said to do.

"Your wings are scorched! I'm amazed you were able to fly home," he said with concern.

"I didn't fly," she said bashfully. "We rode him." Tulip pointed to the pond, where the dog frolicked in the water. Fairies were swarming over him, washing his coat and picking off fleas.

"Wait a minute!" Felicity turned to Opus in shock. "Did you say fiancée?" He nodded, and she jumped over next to him. She wrapped her arms around his neck and smothered him in kisses.

While the surprising revelation was occurring. Solomon brought his attention back to his injured fledgling. "Little one, you must go to Prunella right now, sit down, and let her mend your wings."

"I can't," she said shyly.

"Why can't you?" he asked, surprised at her resistance.

"I can't sit down," she said. "I scorched my fanny too!"

"Oh!" Solomon was a little embarrassed for her, yet you could see the twinkle of a smile start in his eyes. "You poor thing. Maybe you can stand to tend to your injuries."

"But I don't have time. I'm making Felicity's dress," she argued.

"Tend to your injuries first," Solomon said. "Then if Prunella says it's okay, you can make Felicity's dress."

Tulip submitted reluctantly. "Yes, Solomon." She walked away with the measuring tape still dragging behind her. She was frustrated at being treated like a little chick, and under her breath, kicking the ground, and buzzing her wings with each harrumph.

"And no flying until your wings are healed," Solomon yelled after her.

Tulip stopped, turned with her mouth agape, and stomped her foot with a fierce growl. She gave him a piercing stare and stalked off.

"My word," Solomon uttered, taken aback. "I just don't know what's come over Tulip. She has always been very sweet and amiable. Now she seems as fractious as you are, Amelia."

"Yeah, isn't it great? She grew up so much," Amelia said with pride in her eyes.

Opus and Felicity were still hugging during the verbal exchanges and were shocked at how familiarly Amelia and Tulip behaved with the king of trees. Solomon acted more like a loving parent to the fairies than the giant oak tree he was.

"Amelia, why don't you take Opus and Felicity to Prunella?" Solomon suggested. "I believe she is ready with the restorative for both of you. When Prunella is finished with them, I'm sure they would like to clean up. Make sure Tulip goes with you. She seems to have gained some of Prunella's obstinacy and may conveniently forget to bathe." He reached with a limb and pinched his nose. In his bass voice, he added, "And she needs it!"

The group laughed at his joke and went to the cooking area.

Prunella was just finishing bandaging Tulip's rump and applying aloe vera to the burns on her wings when Amelia and the puppets arrived.

Not far away, Julia had settled on a large rock and announced, "You all are doing a fine job. When the work is completed, we will celebrate the arrival of our three new family members."

A cheer arose from the fey folk as they lifted their voices in song and cheerfully returned to work.

"Here." Prunella handed out cups of steaming amber liquid. "All of you drink this and then clean up." They drank the brew and instantly felt the delicious drink invigorate them.

Amelia grabbed a sudsy bucket, brushes, and washcloths. Felicity's hand pulled her toward the pond. Opus trailed after them skeptically and began to frown.

Tulip, watching them leave, sipped her brew slowly. "Prunella, when you're finished, will I be able to sew on Felicity's dress?" She sipped and waited fearfully as her toes wiggled.

Prunella was agitated and out of patience because of all the excitement and lack of sleep. With tiredness she did not intend, she said, "Yes. Yes! Just go and clean up with the rest of them. And try not to get your bandages wet."

Tulip jumped down from her perch and ran after her friends. "And change that smoky jumper you're wearing. It smells," Prunella called after her.

Amelia and Felicity were already neck-deep in the water when Tulip arrived.

Opus was standing at the water's edge, decidedly uncomfortable. He had taken his shoes off. When he placed a toe in the water, he shivered and chattered. "Brrr! Much too cold! I'll just go warm a bucket of water and wash behind those bushes."

He hadn't taken more than two steps when Felicity piped up loudly, "Opus, get back here and wash!" Everyone who was washing and playing close by stopped and stared at Opus, who had become the center of attention.

Trying to act calm, he said, "Oh, that's okay, Felicity. I'll take care of it over there." He pointed over his shoulder to some bushes.

A little push from behind made Opus stumble to the water's edge. "Scaredy frog," he heard Tulip tease.

Turning to face her, he saw Tulip with one hand on her hip and the other pointing toward the pond. "Go on, ya scaredy frog."

Although Tulip was half his size, Opus felt trapped. He quickly looked and pointed to his left, and with a sharp intake of breath, said, "What's that over there?" Tulip and all the fairies in the water looked away as Opus hurried the opposite way.

Opus was quickly surrounded by Dixie and five trooper fairies. They grabbed and lifted him up. Flying to the middle of the pond, they released him, making a big splash. Surfacing, he flailed his arms and legs about wildly, shouting, "I can't swim!"

"No, you can't swim," came the calm voice of Felicity. "But you can float," she added as she slowly drifted over to him.

"Tee hee! Relax, Opus," Tulip encouraged from the shore.

Remembering that wood floats, he was a little miffed and felt foolish. No longer thrashing, he stiffly held his arms at his sides and floated face-up. A bevy of fairies surrounded him with brushes and soap. They scrubbed the soot away, along with much of his old paint.

"We might as well scrub your loose paint off too, Felicity, and get rid of those nasty hair stubs while we're at it!" Amelia rubbed energetically on Felicity's head.

"Be careful, Amelia, or I won't have any finish left," Felicity complained.

"Don't worry," Tulip piped up. "We have plans for you two."

When the puppets were clean, they were given robes to wear. Now sparkling clean, the troop walked back to the cook fires, now bursting with activity. Prunella had finally collapsed, much to the delight of the cooks. A cozy nest had been built up around her, and cotton was stuffed in her ears. A lean-to was erected to shade her from the sun, and white-socks pixies watched over her. Their love and respect were obvious as they ensured she was not disturbed or awakened. Some sang soft lullabies as she happily cuddled her magnifying glass and snoozed.

A short, round fairy shushed everyone with a chubby finger to her lips. She was the head cook, and her name was Cookie. She had rosy cheeks and a square of cloth wrapped around her head.

She carried her large spoon like a sword of judgment, meting out justice equally to slackers, food critics, or the errant finger in her pies. (Between you and me, I wouldn't disparage her cooking.) She ruled over her cook pot with a will of iron, and only Prunella had the force of will to match Cookie's.

When they reached the picnic tables, Cookie sighed and rolled her eyes toward Prunella. "We coaxed her to sit and have some tea," Cookie said. "I spiked it with a little chamomile to relax her, and out she went. Now that, that busybody is out of the way, we professional cooks can finish up." Cookie started to work herself into a real tizzy. She acted like she was the only one who knew how to brew up an infusion. "Well, I ask you who knows better about herbs and spices than a cook? Well?" She waved her spoon at them imperiously.

With trepidation, the troop nodded and voiced agreement. "Why, you do! Yes, yes, cooks know better!"

"Weelll of course I do, and I showed her." She harrumphed. Cookie hugged the handle of the spoon under her arm and rubbed her hands together. "Now, what can I do for you fine young feys?"

"Um, we are kinda hungry, Cookie," Tulip said as she rubbed her tummy.

"Go sit, sit. I'll bring you some porridge." Cookie shooed them to the tables and went back to the cook pots.

They sat down among fairies already in the middle of their breakfasts. Tulip sat on Felicity's right side and looped her arm around Felicity's handless arm. She pulled out some silver wire and a small pair of needle-nose pliers, and proceeded to work on Felicity's hand and arm.

Felicity was distracted and happily unaware as she prattled away, answering the many curious questions the fairies asked her. All the chatter kept her so occupied, she barely noticed when the bowl of porridge appeared in front of her. Between bites, Felicity told her tales or answered everyone's questions about noisy giants.

Nectar was poured into a mug and set in front of her. She picked up the cup and drank thirstily. Setting the cup down, she turned her attention back to the fairies, stories, and questions. She had been looking away and listening intently. Suddenly, her loud squeal startled the entire table. With a surge of feeling, Felicity suddenly realized her right hand had been reattached! She wiggled her fingers and gazed in wonder. It had been so long since she had the use of it. She wondered as she picked up the cup with ease. Felicity took a grape from a bowl and squeezed it with her one hand easily, squishing out all the juice.

"Oh, thank you, thank you, Tulip," Felicity shrieked as she held her with both hands and squeezed tightly. Tulip squeaked joyfully when Felicity gave her loud, smacky kisses all over her face.

Breakfast ended, and the puppets were ushered into separate tents for their makeovers. Hours passed, and finally Opus emerged, looking like a new person. His skin gleamed, there was a twinkle in his eyes, and his dark brown hair was full and real. He cut a dashing figure, wearing a large, plain white pullover shirt with full sleeves. A wide belt circled his waist, accenting his shoulders. His pant legs were cut at two handbreadths below his knees and buttoned at the bottom of the pant leg. Long socks and soft shoes completed his remake, and he looked princely.

Opus felt so invigorated he went over to help hang decorations for the party. As he worked his mind kept returning to the question of why Felicity had not emerged yet from the tent. The tent she was in bustled with activity. When he walked over to ask about her, it sounded like she was having the time of her life in there. He called her name, and the tent immediately went dead quiet. Whispering and giggling ensued. Amelia exited the tent, holding the flaps closed behind her. Small sticks were pinned in her hair, and her face was covered with a lavender-colored paste.

Amelia grinned as though she was hiding a secret. "May I help you?" Her pretty smile shined through her cream-covered face.

"I was wondering how Felicity is doing," Opus replied. He raised his voice and asked, "How ya doing in there, sweetheart?"

A new surge of whispers and giggles followed his question. As he pressed forward to hear what was being said, Amelia put both hands on his chest and pushed him back hard.

"Hey, this is a restricted area," she said sternly. "No visitors allowed, so buzz off." With that, Amelia disappeared back into the tent.

Opus placed his ear to the tent fabric and managed to hear, "Congratulations," and, "You showed him." Before he could open the flap and push his way through, he realized someone had sewed up the entrance.

"Hey, that's not fair," Opus shouted indignantly as he pawed at the entrance without success.

"Opus," Felicity shouted, "this is a girls only tent. We'll be finished when we're finished." Then sweetly she asked, "Would you be a dear and go ask Dixie to come here, please?" More giggles followed.

Opus felt defeated. "Okay, Felicity, but I hope you're not too much longer." There were more giggles as he stalked off with his shoulders slumped. The message to Dixie delivered, he went back to help prepare for the feast. Later, he looked again in the direction of Felicity's tent and saw it was now guarded by a squad of Dixie's protector fairies. With a final scowl, he stalked off to get something to eat.

Dusk fell, firefly lanterns illuminated the celebration grounds, and garlands hung from Solomon's boughs. The limbs seemed to sway back and forth in time to the beautiful music wafting in his branches. Tables were filled with food and guarded by Cookie. Julia, dressed in her finest gown, sat with Opus. He was regaling her with tales of the good times he and Felicity had with their old family so long ago. Julia's gaze shifted behind him, and her eyes twinkled as she smiled at what she saw coming. The music stopped and was replaced by exclamations and gasps. Opus turned and was speechless, his mouth open and eyes wide.

Coming up the path, Felicity was flanked by a parade of ladies in waiting. Amelia and Tulip, splendidly dressed as they were, paled in comparison to

Felicity's radiance. Her gown sparkled in the fireflies' light. A delicate spider web shawl covered her milky shoulders. The most surprising change was the mass of beautiful tresses cascading from her head and embracing her shoulders to the middle of her back. Her hair was now brunette with blonde highlights. Colorful ribbons hung from the garland crowning her head, enhancing the shape of her angelic visage.

Opus rose to greet her and gracefully bowed in courtly fashion. From behind his back he presented a small bouquet of posies he had picked. She sniffed the flowers and blushed.

Whispering loudly, she said, "I see they gave you hair too. The new style makes you look even more handsome than you were. I think I love you even more now."

Opus reddened, boyishly shy but unable to keep from staring in to her lovely eyes.

"What?" Felicity asked. She was smiling and a little concerned that he might not like her new look. She brushed a strand of curls away from her eyes and a little self-consciously asked, "Is it too much?"

"No! I was just." He paused and took her hand in his. "I am, I love you, Felicity."

Felicity glowed with pleasure. She wrapped her arms around his neck and kissed him.

With the two puppets lovingly embracing, Solomon happily announced, "Well, this is the way to start a celebration. Ho, ho, ho." His laughter echoed. "Julia, were you going to say something?" Amelia and Tulip flew up and kissed each of his chubby cheeks.

CHAPTER 14
CELEBRATION

Julia stood, raised her hand for attention, poised her wings, and said, "Dear fey members of the Beaver Valley family, many of you were unable to help with the rescue mission because you gallantly attended to the important work that had to be done here. The mission and its success would not have been possible without you. I thank you, and I know Opus and Felicity thank you.

"For those of you who have not met them yet, let me explain. Opus and Felicity look very much like small noisy giants, but in fact, they were created from abandoned parts of a very close friend of our dear friend Solomon many, many years ago. Opus and Felicity have known love and were part of a family. Then sadly, they were abandoned. Their time together in the old giants' house is where they almost met their ends. Fate intervened by bringing our own Amelia and Tulip into their lives. That is how the rescue mission began. The rescue involved wonderful efforts by many of you. Now, Opus and Felicity, and Liberty will be part of our community. Liberty courageously carried the three of them all the way back to Beaver Valley. You are aware that Tulip was injured and probably could not have flown home."

Julia, smiling, announced, "The addition of Opus and Felicity to our family provides us with a need for a new ceremony. As most of you know, for generations, our colonies have been perpetuated by the mystery of pollen assimilation. We have had no need for the union of couples called marriage as the noisy giants do. Recognizing that many couples unite for life in the human and animal worlds because of enduring love and faith, Solomon and I agree that Felicity and Opus have lived that kind of life and can be united here.

"Opus, Felicity, please step forward. Opus, do you wish to be united with Felicity for the rest of your life?"

Opus unhesitatingly responded, "I certainly do!"

"Felicity, do you wish to be united with Opus for the rest of your life?"

Felicity trembled with emotion and said, "I have always loved Opus and always will. Yes!"

The throng slapped their wings and cheered as Julia pronounced, "May you both live long and happy lives as a united couple. Let the celebration begin!"

Hearing Julia's command, Cookie released her contained enthusiasm and shouted to her excited helpers, "Pansy, Rose, Violet, start the cooking fires, skewer the meat, and pour the juice." Looking around for more help, she saw Sassy lounging near the blueberries and ordered, "Enough sampling. Pull those stems quickly, and then squeeze the lemons!" Then she called, "Nasturtium, Quickly take some helpers, and go get enough nectar for the toasts."

At the edge of the community area, the musical fairies began wiping clear beeswax on the strings of their instruments and polishing the flutes and tambourines.

Fairies darted back and forth from the glen with strings of flowers and other bright decorations. Other fairies shaped and arranged wax gob candles. The entire area bustled with activity. Solomon smiled and relished the pleasure generated by the happy folk.

Even Liberty (a great name for a freedom helper) dashed from group to group of workers, enjoying the spirit of the impending festivities.

Finally, all the activity seemed to stall as Julia was pleased with the result. She called out in a clear soprano voice, "Wonderful, all of you! Now, everyone go clean up, and put on your finest things for the dance. We will light candles and begin the music at dust. Opus and Felicity will begin the evening with a waltz from their days of performing for the noisy giants. A waltz is a slow, graceful sliding motion that some of you will try to learn. Later, there will be nectar for everyone and toasts to the future. Now, hurry and get ready!"

The fairies quickly vacated the beautifully decorated compound. Julia was satisfied it was time to celebrate.

The sun sank below the trees, and the darkness began to creep in. Candles were lit. The warmth of their light chased the darkness away, and the fairies started to sway to the rhythm of the musicians. Felicity was ravishing in her new clothes and the beautiful necklace of sparkling stones. There were even a few of the sparkling stones in her hair. Opus came toward her with obvious adoration in his eyes, bowed, and offered his hand. They smoothly glided in long, sweeping moves with the music. Soon, the fairies followed their actions, and the whole abode appeared to be moving.

At end of the waltz, Solomon rumbled his profound blessing on the entire gathering. Julia glided up to his chin with a shell filled with nectar and poured some on his bark lips. Love abounded. Later, the candles dimmed and went out. They all enjoyed the evening and looked forward to their new life together.

R. S. Rayborn